The Gospel According to

Beauty and the Beast

A Story of Transformation

Mary Scifres

Edited by B. J. Beu

THE GOSPEL ACCORDING TO BEAUTY AND THE BEAST:
A STORY OF TRANSFORMATION

Copyright © 2017 by Mary Scifres

All rights reserved.

DEDICATION

To the beauty that resides within.

PREFACE

Once upon a time. . . . These four short words transport us into a magical land of make believe—a land filled with monsters and heroes, a land of social conformity and epic adventure, a land of hatred and redemptive love. These four short words let us know we are entering a story filled with life and truth, hope and possibility. For in fairy tales, the power of myth emerges, connecting us to ancient truths and elements of the human story that haven't changed since the dawn of time.

Fairy tales have called to me since I was a tiny girl. Their beautiful pictures and magical words continue to mesmerize, inspire, and comfort me today. Even as a child, I knew I would one day fill pages of my own with words. As I became a teenager, fairy tales called to me each Sunday evening as I watched *The Wonderful World of Disney* with my family. As I entered my young adult years, fairy tales called to me through Walt Disney's animated classics and the new stories that came to the screen during the Disney Renaissance of the 1990s. And when our son Michael was born in 1997, fairy tales called to me in a whole new way. Watching his young face light up with joy and hope, seeing his eyes sparkle with dreams and imagination, and hearing his laughter and singing erase the pain of a terrible day at school, only deepened my love for this genre, both in books and on the silver screen.

My love for Disney films grew once more as I recognized that our son is a lover of film in the way that I am a lover of books. The prophet Kahlil Gibran teaches that we can give our children our love, but not our thoughts.[1] I recognized that I could give Michael my love of story, but not my love of books. While Michael enjoyed listening to stories as he cuddled in my lap, their magic came alive for him when we watched them on screen. Disney and Pixar films were staples in our household, and Michael can still recite lines and songs verbatim from his favorites: *The Little Mermaid*, *Monsters Inc,* and, of course, *Beauty and the Beast.* For my husband B. J. and me, our favorite film has long been Disney's *Beauty and the Beast*, and so our young son grew up watching it over and over. I would sing Belle and Mrs. Potts, and he would sing Gaston and Beast, both of us singing the villagers' parts. When he fell in love for the first time, Michael and his girlfriend repeated the pattern: she singing Belle or Ariel or Anna, he singing Beast or Sebastian or Hans and Olaf.

True magic, like true love, lasts a lifetime and only deepens with the passing years. So it was that I discovered this magic in new and surprising ways while attending a 25th anniversary screening of *Beauty and the Beast* at Disney's El Capitan Theatre in Hollywood. Perhaps it was because I was yearning for higher wisdom during a troubled election season. Perhaps it was because I was seeking comfort as an empty nester during my son's freshman year of college. Perhaps it was because I was caught up in the creative energy of like-minded Disney fans who had come to enjoy this classic film while anticipating the soon to be released live action version. Perhaps it was because I was just more attuned to the higher mythological themes that this classic story offers. For whatever reason, as I watched the film, I saw before my eyes a gospel story—a story of good news, a story of self-giving love and life-giving transformation, a story of resurrection and life.

Seeing Belle yearn to discern her call and her father persist in pursuing his dreams; observing Gaston succumb to his narcissistic pursuit of power and popularity and Beast struggle to discover his higher self, I beheld the people of the gospels—people on the journey of self-discovery and transformation. I saw people yearning for relationship—sometimes living into that yearning with love and virtue, other times living into that yearning with selfishness and vice. In the film's story, I recognized the deep yearning for transformation that calls to each one of us. As I watched the transformative power of love change the characters in the story, I wondered just how many lives have been changed by this transformative power since the dawning of time.

In the glorious setting of El Capitan, I saw in *Beauty and the Beast* a reflection of the gospels' portrayal of a man from Nazareth who encountered the best and the worst of human nature, who lived the ancient story of good versus evil to his death and beyond, and who effected personal and communal transformation. In that seeing, the idea for this book emerged. And so, I began to write. As the book grew and developed, as books do, this book has taken on a life of its own. Books are like children; we may conceive them, but they grow in their own right at their own pace into their own creative beings. As this book grew beyond the womb of my first ideas, it became clear that the lessons of *Beauty and the Beast*, like the lessons of the gospels, extend beyond the world of Christianity. These lessons help us explore life truths, question previous assumptions, and glimpse paths toward transformation. In the pages of this book, I offer glimpses of these paths, as I wander through the stories of Belle, Beast, Maurice, Gaston, the villagers, and the castle servants. Most of the book has been inspired by the 1991 animated classic, but it is enhanced and expanded by the recent 2017 live action rendition of the story.

In my musing, I invite you to enjoy your own explorations of meaning and purpose, as you reflect on these stories and re-watch the films. As you read these pages, you will discover your own insights and find your own truths within the story. Like all good stories, the stories of the gospels along with the stories of *Beauty and the Beast* are never really finished—as the stories continue to roll around in our imaginations and the ideas continue to flow through our thoughts, inviting new wisdom, encouraging new hope, and inspiring new journeys toward transformation. That is my hope for this book. That is my hope for you. That is my hope for all who watch these wonderful films and read the transformative stories of the gospels. And so I give you *The Gospel According to Beauty and the Beast: A Story of Transformation.*

ACKNOWLEDGEMENTS

Writing a book is its own transformational journey. On this adventurous and sometimes painful journey, the transformative power of community has helped me reach my destination, and I have many people to thank. First and foremost, I wish to thank my beloved soul mate, husband, best friend, and amazing editor, B. J. Beu. For the countless hours you shared discussing my insights and ideas, for always believing in me and pushing me to be my best, and for the numerous rereads, revisions, and re-writes, I am truly grateful. For our son Michael Beu, who worked tirelessly to help create the cover art and responded time and again to each new request I brought while juggling a busy first year of college, I offer my thanks! This has truly been a family project, and I am indebted to my extended family of parents and siblings for cheering us on along the way.

It takes a village to complete a book, and many friends and colleagues deserve special credit for their part in bringing this book to its final form. To Karen Clark Ristine, who helped with numerous copy edits, shared valuable insights, and always offered an encouraging word, I bestow my humble thanks. I am honored to have the insight of my visionary friend Clara Lee, who read pages, helped with cover art, and always reminded me "You've got this!" For my Marketing Assistant, Andrew Ponder Williams, who cheered me on as we brainstormed how best to get this book into your hands and hearts, I extend joy for our collaboration. Thank you! For those who have laughed and rejoiced with me in this process, who have supported and loved me with your prayers and presence, and who have constantly reminded me to believe that my words and my gifts can inspire and help change the world for the better, thank you! Your belief means more than you will ever know.

And I am especially grateful to you, dear reader, for entering my world. Thank you for celebrating the gifts of these timeless tales, and exploring the lessons they teach. Here's to your personal journeys of transformation. Here's to your journeys of communal transformation. And here's to the world's journey of transformation. May we one day all look back and say, "And they all lived happily ever after!"

TABLE OF CONTENTS

PROLOGUE

Walt Disney's *Beauty and the Beast* is first and foremost a story of transformation, which is fitting, since the story itself has undergone countless transformations over the centuries. While Disney borrowed heavily from the well-known 18th century French fairy tale, "La Belle et le Bête" by Jeanne-Marie Leprince de Beaumont for the 1991 film, the 2017 live-action version remains closest to the original.

Both Disney adaptations of *Beauty and the Beast* begin with a prologue, narrating a tragic story of a selfish young prince who answers the door on a stormy night to find a haggard, old woman offering a single rose in exchange for shelter for the night. Sneering at the gift, the prince dismisses the old woman, even though she warns the boy not to be "deceived by appearances, for beauty is found within."[2] When the prince dismisses her a second time, the old woman's unsightly appearance fades away, revealing a beautiful enchantress where the old crone had been. Despite the prince's repeated apologies, the enchantress perceives a young man with no love in his heart. And so, she casts a spell on the young prince, along with his castle and all its inhabitants, leaving him with a magical rose and an ominous warning: Unless he can learn to love and earn another's love before the rose's last petal falls, the prince will be condemned to live as a beast forever, and the castle servants will, in turn, remain magical household objects, never to return to their human form. If, however, the prince learns to love and finds love in return, the curse will be broken.

With only a few petals remaining on the rose, our story begins. In a darling French village, our would-be princess, Belle, strolls from her father's cottage through the streets of her town, singing of her provincial town and of her dreams of a larger life, as her neighbors sing of this strange, but beautiful girl in their midst. The village heartthrob, Gaston, interrupts Belle's song of longing to remind her that he is the handsome man who can make her dreams come true; Belle skirts his advances and returns to her father Maurice, who is an eccentric inventor in the 1991 animated classic, and a melancholy artisan in the 2017 version. Soon, Maurice hitches up his horse, Philippe, to a wagon and is on his way out of town with his handiwork, as Belle continues to sing of her dreams and hopes for a larger, more creative future.

Maurice, however, gets lost in the woods and is chased by wolves to the gates of an enchanted castle where he encounters Beast, never imagining that this beastly master of the castle is actually a handsome prince in disguise. Beast casts Maurice into a tower prison cell, while Philippe returns home alone. Seeing the horse without wagon and rider, Belle knows her father is in distress, and asks Philippe to help her find him. Upon arriving at the dark castle, Belle hesitantly enters the main hall to search for her father. When she finds him imprisoned, frightened, cold, and alone, Belle is determined to rescue him. Even when she meets the hideous Beast, Belle demands her father's release and then offers herself in exchange for his freedom. With this act of self-sacrifice, a very different story emerges.

Beast sends Maurice home without a backward glance, demanding in return that Belle remain as his prisoner forever. Eager to break the spell on the castle, Beast's servants convince him to house Belle in a beautiful castle suite and encourage him to treat her as an honored guest. Beast's temper and temperament do not respond well to Belle's sullenness and resistance to his overtures to join him for dinner, and soon the two are at odds, Beast going so far as refusing her food unless she dines with him. Beast further forbids Belle from visiting the West Wing where his rose is sheltered in his personal chambers. Later on that first evening, however, the inquisitive Belle enjoys an enchanted, musical dinner and a castle tour, hosted by Cogsworth the steward-turned-mantle-clock along with Lumiere the maître d'-turned-candelabra, and Mrs. Potts the house-keeper-turned-teakettle. The ever-inquisitive Belle sneaks away from her hosts to explore the forbidden West Wing, where she again inflames Beast's anger and in turn runs away from the castle.

While escaping through the forest, Belle is attacked by a pack of wolves, only to be saved by Beast who has followed her into the woods—perhaps to observe, perhaps to protect. In saving Belle, Beast is wounded. With freedom before her, Belle chooses to save Beast's life, returning him to his castle, where she gently dresses his wounds and courageously demands he control his temper. Amazingly, a friendship is formed, and the two begin dining, reading, talking, and playing together. The servants look on with wonder, awe, and hope. Perhaps Belle truly is the one who will teach the prince how to love and be loved, and thus break the spell.

Just as their love begins to blossom and they enjoy an enchanted evening of romantic dining and dancing, Beast offers Belle her freedom when she expresses grief at missing her father. Belle leaves the castle again, this time at Beast's invitation, to return home to her father, who has been desperately trying to return to the castle to save her. Belle returns home to find Gaston awaiting her return, insisting she marry him if she wishes to save Maurice from being imprisoned in an insane asylum for raving about a beast in a castle.

This series of events quickly takes an unexpected turn of events when Belle tries to save her father by revealing Beast's presence in a magic mirror. In trying to convince Gaston and her village that Maurice is neither fiction nor crazy, Belle infuriates Gaston, who stirs up the village's fear with tales of a dangerous beast who will threaten their home and families. Locking up Belle and Maurice, Gaston and the villagers march to attack the castle.

Once Belle and her father escape, Belle rushes back to Beast and finds the castle under attack. While the servants bravely defend the castle against the invading villagers, Beast forlornly allows Gaston and the villagers to overtake him and his home, thinking Belle has decided not to return to him. When Belle witnesses Gaston's attack and begs him for mercy, Beast regains hope and overcomes Gaston's attack, even as his servants oust the villagers. In an act of mercy and kindness, Beast releases Gaston, commanding him to leave the castle and never return. Just as Beast and Belle reach out to joyously reunite in friendship, Gaston cowardly attacks Beast from behind, falling to his own death in the process, but not before mortally wounding Beast. As the last rose petal falls and Beast succumbs to death, Belle finally realizes her deep love for this unusual creature. Her love breaks the spell, resurrecting the dead Beast and transforming him back into a handsome prince. As the prince's outer appearance changes to reflect the inwardly loving man he has become, the entire castle is also transformed to beauty, light, and human form. Well, except for a cute footstool, who becomes an even cuter shaggy dog, complete with happy barks and joyous bounces. In true Disney style, Belle and her now-handsome prince, surrounded by their loving community of castle servants and father Maurice, dance into their happily ever after, and their classic tale is ended with joy and love.

TRANSFORMATION:
THE HEART OF THE STORY

The journey toward life-giving transformation calls to each of us. We are intrigued by those who reveal new paths and new possibilities—the growing child, the imaginative inventor, the creative artist, and the courageous explorer. When we yearn to be more, to do more, and to achieve more, we are hearing that call. When we yearn to love more deeply, live more fully, and think more expansively, the call is pulling us toward the transformation that will allow us to love, live, and think in beautiful new ways. And as we love, live, and think in beautiful new ways, these very acts of loving, living, and thinking transform us, spurring us to even greater transformation. Such is the story of *Beauty and the Beast*. Such is the story of the gospels. For they are stories that heed the call to life-giving change—stories that portray the power of transformation, and the paths toward life-giving transformation upon which we are meant to walk.

FOUNDATIONAL STORIES

Stories that heed the call to life-giving change are the stories that give our lives orientation and meaning. These are the stories that support the spiritual houses of our very being—stories at the foundation of our lives, reaching deep into the darkness and mystery beneath consciousness. Such stories shape and arrange perceptions, revealing patterns and meaning. They change our perspective, inviting us to think differently or notice new things. They strengthen our hope and encourage our love, inviting us to nurture hope and love within others. Our foundational stories are like the pilings of the gabled houses on the canals in Amsterdam, which would have sunk long ago in the sand and mud if not for the pilings upon which they stand. Foundational stories make us capable of love and sacrifice, and illuminate the path to the kingdom of God within us and around us. Foundational stories, like *Beauty and the Beast*, reveal the power of and path toward personal and communal transformation, which is the power and path of the gospel.

Transformation lies at the heart of this fairy tale. From the story's very beginning, when a mysterious enchantress changes a boy-prince without love in his heart into a hideous beast, to the story's conclusion, when the beast is transformed back into human form after learning to give and receive love, transformation marks the milestones of this tale. Those who are tired of the old Disney formula—boy meets girl, boy and girl fall in love, boy and girl overcome obstacles, boy and girl live happily ever after—will be pleasantly surprised by the complexity and depth of this tale. In one sense, this follows the traditional boy meets girl trope, yet our story begins in tragic fashion with the boy and his castle twisted by a terrible spell. The boy doesn't seem to stand a chance, and likely wouldn't, if the heart of this tale was about romantic love, rather than the type of love that leads to a transformation of the soul. *Beauty and the Beast* reveals that the key to unlocking hope, reclaiming joy, and attaining fulfillment on the journey of life is rooted in personal and communal transformation.

The Need for TRANSFORMATION

The journey of life is a story in and of itself, and if the story of this journey is to form the pilings to support our spirit, it must be one of transformation. Every stage of growth invites us to yet another stage of growth. Conflicts and turmoil arise in need of resolution. Relationships emerge, fade, or change, offering additional opportunities for growth and transformation. We are never finished products. With each goal we achieve, we discover new goals ahead. With each turn of the path, we find another fork in the road that demands we choose our course. Will we take the well-worn path that countless others have walked before us, no matter how uninspiring it might be, or will we take the road less travelled?

Being transformed into a beast is certainly taking the road less travelled, but the prince's journey was by another's design, not his own. Sometimes the road we find ourselves walking is nothing like the road we would choose. In Beast's case, it is the result of a seemingly tragic spell cast by a mysterious visitor. But what if this spell is more gift than curse? What if the mysterious visitor is bringing unexpected blessings or even an opportunity for transformation? Throughout history and across literary genres, angelic visitors and tragic situations have invited more than just despair. They symbolize the unknown, the mysterious, even the hero's journey. They are just as likely to be connected to mysterious opportunity and cosmic purpose as they are to tragedy and disaster. In our tale's opening narration, mysterious and tragic though it may be, something mysterious and mystical is clearly afoot, which just may bring something wonderful in its wake.

Jesus' entry into the world is no less mysterious. It's a tale filled with wonder and awe—a tale tinged with promise. His story starts off on a shaky note, with an unwed pregnancy and a long journey ending with no room at the inn. But then comes the magical night of his birth. Heralded by angels and shepherds, wise men and a guiding star, Jesus' mystical entry into the world surely suggests a life of blessing and fortune to come. If any story is set up to have a happy ending, it is the story of Jesus. But no sooner is this divine child born than he and his family face danger and murderous intent. Events and outcomes are difficult to predict based upon their beginnings. And so it is with Beast. His luxurious beginning as a young prince quickly takes a seemingly disastrous turn when he is changed into a beast. Even as the spell takes hold, we wonder what beautiful transformation might be in store if and when this cursed prince finally learns to love, and another learns to love him in return.

Jesus' beginnings are plagued with every bit as much mystery, confusion, and peril. Jesus' mother, Mary, is almost cast out by her fiancé, Joseph, when he finds his young bride-to-be pregnant. Even after an angelic messenger convinces Joseph that Mary's child was conceived by God, the couple must surely have been looked upon with disdain and distrust for this unwed pregnancy. When traveling to Joseph's home-town of Bethlehem, they are not invited to stay with family members, even though Mary is about to give birth. Left out in the cold, they turn to a busy inn, where the only shelter they can find to bear their child is in a stable, meant to stable beasts. Surrounded by animals and visited by dirty shepherds, the holy family begins their story in humiliating circumstances. Their story only grows more tragic when King Herod seeks to kill the boy, and his family is forced to flee to faraway Egypt.

From the very beginning, the story of Jesus is the story of a world in need of transformation. This is a world where families reject one another when rules are broken or reputations tarnished. This is a world where leaders harm the innocent and the powerless in order to protect their power, position, and wealth. This is a world where travelers and immigrants, even young mothers and children, are turned away with a closed door and a hardened heart, regardless of their peril. This is a

7

world in need of transformation—a world very like our fairy tale, *Beauty and the Beast.*

THE TRANSFORMATIVE POWER OF LOVE

From the very beginning, Beast's curse invites us onto a higher level of thought and spiritual inquiry. Beast is not just another handsome prince seeking true love with a beautiful princess. While no one will confuse Beast's beginnings with great religious leaders like Jesus, and few would equate Beast's journey with mythic heroes like Perseus, Beast's beginnings and heroic quest are mysterious and magical, if not other-worldly. This is a special person, sought out by a mysterious visitor and put under a magical enchantment. This is a man-beast in need of transformation, a special child in search of the deepest spiritual lesson of all—the lesson of love. The 2017 film portrays a young prince who has been surrounded by a community in need of transformation: servants who enable his selfishness and depravity, while failing to protect him from ruination at the hands of his father; nobility within the castle who revel in the luxurious parties thrown at the expense of the poor peasants who are taxed unjustly.

Just as there are four gospel accounts in scripture of Jesus' birth, life, death, and resurrection, there are many versions of *Beauty and the Beast.* But at the heart of each of the Disney renditions lies this spiritual truth—to live a fully human life, one must see beyond appearances and one must extend love beyond oneself. We need to love generously and compassionately, and even give selflessly and sacrificially, if we are to embrace the life-giving transformation available to us through the power of love. This lesson lies at the heart of our story, for it is Beast's only hope to transform into the man and prince he is meant to be. This lesson lies at the heart of the gospels as well, for they are stories of transformation that always begin with the power of love.

Jesus teaches and speaks often of love, naming love of God and love of neighbor as the first and greatest commandments. Indeed, Jesus says that those who do not love do not know God, for God is love.[3] Practicing what he preaches, Jesus himself always acts out of love: interrupting travel plans to stop and heal someone, calling to a man hiding in a tree and a woman touching his garment to end her suffering, feeding thousands after a long day of teaching and preaching, calming a storm when he most needs a nap, saving a beloved friend from the grave, and weeping over Jerusalem for rejecting God's compassionate love. There are perhaps no more life-changing love stories ever told than the gospel stories of Jesus—stories of God's incarnate love for the world. But all love stories have transformative power, even and especially when that power is woven into a child's fairy tale.

Love stories change us. Whether they are romantic love stories, friendship love stories, family love stories, or faith community love stories, love stories tap into hidden longings that connect our souls with something larger and more beautiful—something richer and far deeper than our ordinary, everyday existence. The love story of *Beauty and the Beast* is no different. Watching the story of *Beauty and the Beast* unfold on screen changes how we define beauty and ugliness. We grow to love this monstrous looking creature named Beast, despite his appearance. We imagine Mrs. Potts to be a beloved teacher or mother figure, despite the cold, ceramic pottery that encases her nurturing spirit. We admire Belle's spirit and her yearning to expand beyond the limitations of her provincial village. We see not just a beautiful Disney princess, we perceive a hero who can be the one who will learn to love a beast.

While the townsfolk praise and sing of Belle's physical beauty, it is her inner beauty, her loving nature, that make her truly worthy of the name Belle. She is joyous and inquisitive, kind and polite, yet fearless in demanding the best from others. From her first appearance on screen, we see a young woman of friendliness and sweetness, as well as spunk and courage. We easily fall in love with Belle's clever wit and beautiful compassion, not to mention her lovely appearance and lilting voice. She exemplifies the very heart and mind, attitude and behavior, that the enchantress found missing in the young prince. Belle is an easy character to admire and love. The prince? Not so much.

HOW CAN ONE LOVE A BEAST?

How then do we also fall in love with Beast? He is clunky and frightening, overgrown and strange. But thanks to the gift of great story-telling, we also know that inside is a young man yearning to find himself again—a man longing to awaken the human spirit within, a man hoping to transform into the princely ruler he was created to be. Perhaps we see a truth of our own lives in Beast—that we are all both beautiful and ugly inside. Perhaps we recognize that we too experience times of great awareness and expansive understanding, but also times when we sleepwalk through life or neglect opportunities to grow. We too have tasted the life-giving power of loving fully and freely, but also the destructive force of selfishness, jealousy and anger. We are never just one or the other, all Beauty or all Beast. There is always room for growth, always need for additional transformation. For even at our most beautifully loving moments, we are not perfect, and we know that less elevated moments may soon follow. The prince-turned-beast is not all that different than we are at our worst. It is perhaps this awareness that draws us to him.

Beast's deep yearning drives both his hope and his despair. Even when he explodes in anger, he yearns for his better self. I have known this deep yearning in my own life. It is when my thoughts or actions turn ugly that I most yearn to be beautiful. It is when I become hateful that I most ache to be loving. It is when I am stuck inside a hideous pattern of cruelty, self-destruction, or self-absorption that I most deeply long to forge new paths of compassion, abundant life, and selfless love. Beast tugs at my heartstrings because I too have turned away strangers in need of care; I too have mistreated people based on appearances; I too have passed judgment, rather than offering acceptance and love. The truth of the human story is that we are complex creatures with the potential for both love and hate, kindness and cruelty. Yet, beauty always lies within. Within each one of us, a light strives to burst forth with the trans-formative power of love—a light that strengthens us and awakens us to the beauty seeking to flow freely and fully within us.

Under the enchantress' spell, Beast's beauty lies dormant, and his estate lies trapped in endless winter. The glistening snow and ice, with their beautiful fractals of shimmering light, misdirect us from a terrible truth—endless winter hardens the soil and the heart, choking off the potential for growth and new life. In the original fairy tales, this is more clearly explained. In those stories, Beast's rose bush, a cruel reminder of his rejection of the enchantress' gift, is the only living thing in a castle frozen in silence. Beast surely knows that until his frozen heart thaws, his estate will remain in its wintery prison, on a slow journey towards death. And yet, Beast yearns for life—human life and even love—more passionately with each passing day as his friendship with Belle begins to thaw the heart he has locked away.

In the 2017 film, Belle seems to perceive this truth, as she reads a poem during their stroll along the glistening winter lake:

But in that solemn silence
is heard the whisper
of every sleeping thing
Look, look at me!

Come, wake me up!
For still here I be.[4]

As we behold the prince within Beast whispering to be heard, we grow to love both Belle and her prince-beast friend. As our perception is transformed by a story that captures and captivates us, we too start to hear the whisper of our better selves, lying within. Hearing this whisper, we are invited to a further transformation of perspective, attitude, and behavior. We join Belle and Beast on their journeys to look beyond appearances.

Though our eyes tell us it is Beast's physical form that is in need of transformation, a deeper look reveals that the enchantress has merely made the prince's outer visage reflect his inner cruelty. It is his heart that must be transformed for the castle's current tragedy to become future comedy, for today's sorrow to become tomorrow's joy, and for hope to overcome despair. From the 2017 film, we discover that this beastly man was once an innocent child who loved his mother and imagined a future of love and laughter, not the nightmare he currently endures. Unlike *The Princess and the Frog*, no kiss from a beautiful princess can turn Beast back into a handsome prince so they can live happily ever after. As the child-prince and castle servants sing the poignant ensemble, "Days in the Sun," we know that this prince and his castle must be transformed from within if anyone's "ever after" has a chance of being happy. In their song of yearning, we hear the voices of hope and love, reminding us that transformation is always possible.

For light to shine once more, Beast must not only remember former days in the sun as a child, he must be able to imagine days of love and hope to come. Light must shine if the current darkness is to be transformed into light. Only the transformation of Beast's attitude and behavior can effect the final physical transformation that will break the enchantress' spell and allow Beast to become Prince and his castle servants to become human again. His dark despair must give way to hope; his ugly temper must give way to love. All must begin with the transformation of heart and mind.

TRANSFORMATION'S INNER JOURNEY

Such transformation begins within. As we nourish the divine light that resides within, and as we give our time and attention to the best parts of ourselves, we feed and strengthen the beauty inside that longs to shine forth. On the other hand, if we focus on external appearances and neglect the beauty within, we may lose our way, and our light may dim.

A Cherokee parable about two wolves dramatizes this point. "A terrible fight is going on inside me," an old Cherokee chief told his grandson. "There are two wolves constantly at war with each other. One wolf brings death and destruction. He is anger, fear, envy, sorrow, regret, greed, arrogance, self-pity, guilt, resentment, lies, false pride, and ego. The other wolf brings life and renewal. He is joy, peace, love, hope, serenity, humility, kindness, generosity, compassion, and faith. This same fight is going on inside you, and every other person too." The grandson gazed in fear at his grandfather before asking, "Which wolf will win?" The old chief sat in silence for a moment before answering: "The one you feed."

Beauty and the Beast reveals a stark truth about personal and communal transformation; it begins with a choice: Which wolf will we choose to feed? Will we feed the wolf that is good and does no harm—a wolf of love and light, a wolf who walks gently on their earth, taking what it needs for sustenance and fighting only when it is necessary and just? Or will we feed the wolf that is a beast—a wolf full of anger and self-absorption; a wolf that snarls and howls at every little disturbance; a wolf that growls and snaps even at his own family? This wolf fights everyone who challenges him or gets in his way. Often, this wolf fights for no reason at all. She pounces on her prey, even when she is not hungry, and digs up beautiful flowers simply to create chaos. It is pointless behavior, for this angry wolf is never satisfied or restful. These two wolves struggle within each of us for control and dominance. We sense and yearn for the beauty of the kindly wolf, but the powerful anger of the beastly wolf also calls to us. "Which one will win?" the frightened boy asks his grandfather, a masterful storyteller. "The one we feed," he and every other spirit-guide answer back.

Jesus knew this truth that transformation emerges from within, and that we either feed or starve the transformation journey, depending on where we focus our attention. When traveling among religious leaders who strictly observed Jewish law while ignoring the heart of Jewish spiritual life, Jesus chided them for focusing more on the letter of the law than the spirit of love upon which the law was based. Jesus understood that loving God and loving your neighbor as yourself is the summation of scripture, the whole of the Torah—everything else is commentary.[5] Such understanding made Jesus yearn for a world where people act from the wellspring of love—a world where people see the divine image within one another, a world where divine light shines brightly in faith communities with warmth and love for all. Instead, he lived in a world where religious and political leaders focused on the external appearance of righteousness, rather than the inner beauty and transformative power of love. When his disciples were criticized for eating with unwashed hands, as required by Jewish law, Jesus replied:

> Listen to me, everyone, and understand this. Nothing outside a person can defile them by going into them. Rather, it is what comes out of a person that defiles them. . . . For it is from within, out of a person's heart, that evil thoughts come. . . . All these evils come from inside and defile a person.[6]

And when the religious leaders continued to criticize Jesus and his disciples for healing and working on the Sabbath, Jesus responded:

> Woe to you, teachers of the law and Pharisees, you hypocrites! You clean the outside of the cup and dish, but inside they are full of greed and self-indulgence. Woe to you, teachers of the law and Pharisees, you hypocrites! You are like whitewashed tombs . . . on the outside you appear to people as righteous but on the inside you are full of hypocrisy and wickedness.[7]

Jesus looks always for the inner beauty, the inward purity that comes from love. Looking beyond the deceptive outer appearance to perceive the true inner being allows us to see true beauty (or true ugliness). Nourishing our inner beauty creates all the external beauty we will ever need. This message is at the core of the story of *Beauty and the Beast*. While Gaston focuses on his outer beauty, he feeds his inner beast and misses the inner journey that could transform him into a truly handsome man. While Beast worries that his outer appearance will repulse Belle, it is only as his inner warmth shines forth that she begins to appreciate and enjoy his presence in her life. Just as Jesus' taught, both Belle and Beast have to learn that it is what comes from within not without that determines who we are. What is truly transformative is always internal, not external. The beast or beauty we feed within our souls becomes who we are.

A COMPLICATED JOURNEY

Much as I love the 1991 film that stole my heart so many years ago, I am challenged by the complexity of the characters in the 2017 rendition. In the live-action film, we are vividly reminded that even the

13

seemingly perfect Belle has room for growth and transformation. When she first meets Beast, Belle seems both curious and frightened. Even as her curiosity and courage grow, she is not about to extend kindness to a creature who imprisoned her father and now holds her captive. This is not a story of a victim falling in love with her captor, or of unconditional love blindly extended, or of a sudden revelation and overnight transformation. This is a story of the gradual growth of love—a story of the expansion of our heart, mind and soul, when we allow the transformative power of love to broaden our perspective, change our perceptions, improve our attitudes and behaviors, and invite new possibilities into our lives.

Already a curious and creative woman, Belle will need to expand her perspective and change her perceptions if she is to understand this strange new world in which she resides, let alone see the beauty within this beast who has taken her prisoner. As kind and loving as Belle is by nature, she has room to grow in her loving compassion, as we all do. For we are never finished products, as long as we are walking and breathing. We are woven into life's messy journey, moving forward and stepping backward, but ultimately, as Richard Rohr has said, "falling upward."[8] Although Beast and Belle fail plenty of times in their journey of self-discovery, they end up falling upward in the powerful transformation of love—a transformation that sees beyond appearances, gives of itself selflessly, and expresses itself without limits.

Such a journey takes time, and the journey's success requires more than an openness to love, it requires an openness to hope as well. For hope in the midst of despair has a power all its own. Hope leads us to imagine something better. Hope feeds the beauty within, fostering and strengthening our faith. Hope invites us to dream of possibilities that seem impossibly ridiculous. Hope changes our perspective and encourages new perceptions. Hope whispers in our ears that we are more than just the beasts that others perceive, and that our lives can be more than the circumstances that seem to imprison us. Hope breaks the chains that bind us, freeing us to perceive open doors and new paths we hadn't noticed before.

In Beast's first encounters with Belle and her father, we can already see that Beast does have a heart of hope, hesitant though that hope may be. As he watches Belle and discusses her with his servants, Beast hopes that Belle might just be the one to break the spell. Perhaps there is even a loving heart buried within this man-beast. Filled with the stirrings of hope, Beast listens to his servants with gratitude and interacts with them respectfully, in the way one would expect of a good, loving king or master in 18th century France. His years alone in the castle, with only his servants-turned-household-items to keep him company, seem to have laid the foundation for a transformed life.

Still, we may wonder why these servants remain so loyal in the face of such a terrible curse. When Belle wonders the same, advising her new friends that they had done nothing to deserve their fate, Mrs. Potts sadly confirms that they had indeed "done nothing," and thereby deserve their fate. They had done nothing when the prince's mother died and his father treated him cruelly. They had done nothing when the young master grew selfish and cruel as he endured his pain. The enchantress' spell gave them an opportunity to "do something" to help effect the transformation they all need. And so, we meet a prince-beast who is already kinder and gentler than the one who had refused the enchantress' entreaty for shelter so many years before.

Even so, he is an ill-tempered master, quick to express anger and to yell at the slightest provocation. Lacking self-control, Beast seemingly exerts no effort to moderate this poor pattern of behavior. He is an insensitive and self-absorbed captor who only extends hospitality at his servants' prompting. It's no wonder that even after offering herself as prisoner, Belle does not accept Beast's grudging hospitality. She sees only a monster, a cruel captor whom she never intends to befriend or forgive. Meanwhile, even as Beast knows how very much he needs this young woman, if the spell is ever to be broken, he quickly establishes a wall between them with his angry demands and his rude behavior. Belle sees not only what her eyes tell her to perceive, but also what Beast seemingly wants her to perceive: He is a powerful beast, a cruel ruler, and a demanding master who expects obedience and subservience. It would take a very unusual person indeed to see beyond the beast he has become, and Belle is not yet *that* unusual. Beast is no fool when he predicts that Belle will never see him as anything but a monster. For all she initially sees *is* a beast, and Belle has no intention of being a beast's dinner companion, let alone friend.

THE WISDOM OF GOD, NOT THE WORLD, LEADS TO TRANSFORMATION

This is the human story. We trust our instincts, our wisdom, and our experience to guide us, but often let our prejudices determine who is worthy of our attention, compassion, and kindness. Limited by our perceptions and perspectives, we fail to see what lies just beneath the surface, and so we are prone to misjudge others and draw conclusions from the wrong data. We continue on familiar pathways, trusting in the "tried and true" or "straight and narrow." We miss new pathways and alternate routes that could lead to new discoveries and untold growth. We congratulate ourselves on our worldliness and lack of naïveté, thereby shutting ourselves off from the possibility that we might be completely mistaken about things that seem so clear. Jesus turns this worldly wisdom on its head with his teaching to focus on heavenly things rather than earthly things. Build up a storehouse of heavenly treasure, not earthly possessions. Focus on divine things, not human things, or you might just lose your way.[9] Jesus goes even further on this seemingly illogical journey, teaching that we are responsible to offer compassion and kindness even to those we deem unworthy. Jesus calls us to change both perspective and perception in our interactions and judgments of others. Loving your friends isn't enough. Anyone can do that. Love your enemies! Don't just help those who've helped you. Help a stranger lying in the ditch by the road, even a stranger who disgusts or frightens you. No wonder Paul later points out that the wisdom of the cross seems like foolishness to the world.[10]

These teachings of Jesus are foolish by any logical and worldly reasoning. And yet, this crazy, upside-down perspective of Jesus lays bare the path toward transformation. Love those who do you wrong. Expect the best from people who seem the worst. See the beauty within a beast, and discover a new path forward. Look beyond the craggy lines of an old woman's face to seek the wisdom within. Search for the blessing within a curse. See every person as a divine child of love and light, no matter what they might look like or how they might act.

Paul was the right teacher to point out the upside down nature of Jesus' wisdom teachings, for he was living proof that Christ chooses the foolish of the world to be instruments of God's wisdom and recipients of God's transforming love. Long before Paul was deemed a saint of the Church, he was even more of a beast to the fledgling Christian community than the spoiled prince was to the enchantress in disguise. A cruel persecutor of those first followers of Jesus, Paul zealously sought to stamp out the new faith. But on a journey to Damascus, Paul was struck blind and instructed by Jesus' heavenly voice to leave his campaign of persecution behind and become a faithful follower. This famous Christian evangelist and author of much of the New Testament did not begin as an apostle or even a disciple of Christ. Having never

16

met Jesus, Paul was a Pharisee who had hunted, tortured, and possibly even murdered some of Jesus' first and most faithful followers. Still, the risen Christ deemed this beastly man not only worthy of attention, compassion, and kindness, but also worthy of transformation into something greater and more beautiful. The Apostle Paul is living proof that the transformative love of God not only has the power to change lives, it has the power to change the world. We all partake of this power when we embrace the fullness of loving God and neighbor, and when we receive the fullness of God's love for ourselves.

Jesus makes it clear, particularly in the Gospel of Matthew, that loving God and neighbor extends far beyond just loving the neighbors we know and like. After all, anyone can do that. Many of the most hateful and cruel leaders in history have loved and been loved by close family members and friends. Jesus teaches that love extends to the "other," the "stranger," and even the "enemy." Only this type of radically inclusive, self-giving love has the power to transform us, our communities, and even the world. This is the lesson that both Beast and Belle must learn before their inner journey toward transformation can begin. And this is the very type of love that both Beast and Belle must discover within themselves before they can perceive the true beauty that lies within each other.

THE WALLS BLOCKING TRANSFORMATION

This sounds great in theory. And in most fairy tales, the love between prince and princess comes rather quickly, often with as brief an encounter as "true love's kiss." However, we know from experience that true love, deep love, and particularly, selfless love, seldom comes quickly or easily. This is particularly true when it comes to loving the "other," the "stranger," or the "enemy." And such is the case for both Belle and Beast. Belle's stubborn independence initially establishes a wall to protect herself. Beast's temper creates an even stronger fortress, one that seems to prove he is not worthy of love. Certainly, Belle is neither enamored with nor appreciative of this cruel captor known as Beast. She gathers her strength to withstand any demand he might make, and willfully resists any overture that would torment her further. Belle's strength and courage will help her withstand imprisonment, but these qualities must extend to her capacity for compassion and kindness if she is to move beyond the boundaries that box her in, much less break down Beast's wall of anger. For that to happen, Belle will need to see with a new perspective. Both Belle and Beast must at least peek over their self-protective walls if they are to look at one another and discover that they are both much more than they first appear to be.

They both glance tentatively at one another—Beast reflecting on whether this young woman might be "the one" to break the spell, and Belle questioning this Beast's cold-hearted actions as she negotiates for time with her father. Even after a hostile exchange of words over a refused dinner invitation, Belle's curiosity leads her to Beast's private West Wing. There, she explores monster-like statues, a slashed painting of a handsome prince, and an enchanted rose under protective cover. Just when Belle might have begun to break through a bit of Beast's self-protection, Beast responds with fury to her disobedience and the threat he perceives to his rose. In response, Belle responds with courageous pluck by escaping the castle, forsaking the agreement she had made earlier when she bartered for her father's release.

As she seeks to return home, it is only after wolves attack Belle in the forest and Beast and Belle join forces to fight off them off, that they begin to see each other in a new light. Only after shared danger and forced vulnerability with each other are Belle and Beast willing to consider lowering the barriers they had erected to protect themselves. When the wolves turn angrily on Beast as he fights to save Belle's life, Belle must, in turn, save Beast's life. Only when they have both sacrificed self-interest for each other are Belle and Beast able to perceive the connection they share—the connection that each one of us shares with every other created being in this diverse realm of God's creation. Only as they live into this connection, stumbling back to the castle together and mending their battle wounds, are these two unlikely companions able to begin lowering the walls they have built. The seeds of transformation have been planted. Enemies might just become friends after all.

BLESSINGS COME AT THE END

The next stage of the story is a beautiful one, but its beauty should not overshadow the hard journey it took to get here. Indeed, this joyous part of the story is a poignant reminder that we might never reach this stage when we build walls where bridges are most needed. We miss the blessings to come if we run away from challenges, troubles, and even curses that confront us. One of scripture's greatest lessons is that blessings come at the end, after faithful struggle. Abraham had to leave his homeland and become a wandering Aramean before he could become the father of nations through whom all the nations of the world would be blessed. Jacob had to struggle with an angel and suffer a dislocated hip before the angel would bless him and rename him Israel. The Hebrews had to walk out of Egypt and cross the Red Sea while being pursued by Pharaoh's soldiers before God gave them the Ten Commandments on Mount Sinai. Jesus had to endure forty days of hunger and temptation in the wilderness before he could embark on his ministry of healing and hope. And he had to struggle alone in the garden of Gethsemane while his disciples slept, and endure ridicule, betrayal, denial, and death on a cross, before he could be glorified on Easter.

Those who give up too quickly endure life's trials and tribulations without discovering the blessings that are available on the other side. We miss opportunities for transformation if we close our minds to new possibilities or insist on sticking with the familiar paths of our past. Had Beast not ventured out of the castle and into the forest to save Belle's life, he would have likely remained a beast for all time, nursing his anger and his regrets alone in the West Wing of his enchanted castle. He might never have discovered the power of sacrificing for the sake of another. He might never have learned the beauty of learning to love.

Had Belle returned home, she and her father would have likely continued in the very provincial life that felt like imprisonment to the open-minded, imaginative Belle. Beast would have either died in the forest or fallen into even deeper despair, trapped in his beastly form indefinitely. Must we always wait for the wolves of this world to chase us into vulnerability and new ways of seeing? In the Gospel of John, Jesus declares that he has come to offer not only life, but abundant life.[11] We are created for expansive love and abundant life, not for loneliness and despair. We are created for relationship and for creativity, not for isolation and limitation. Often in life, we wait for the disastrous moments before opening ourselves to the transformation that expansive love provides. Journeying through the forests of trials and tribulations can help us embrace new beginnings and life-giving change. But journeying courageously on the path of self-giving love can help effect the same transformation. In *Beauty and the Beast*, both journeys were necessary for these two stubborn souls to peak over their self-protective walls, open themselves to new perspectives and perceptions, and build a bridge of friendship, compassion, and understanding. Both journeys were necessary for these two stubborn souls to find life-changing love and transformations.

19

TRANSFORMATION'S EBB AND FLOW

In the gospels, we see this same transformative power of love bring healing and hope to individuals and communities that were touched by Jesus. But we also see that the transformative power of love ebbs and flows. With two wolves struggling within us, we are both beauty and beast, and our journeys of transformation are seldom in a straight line. For every two steps forward Jesus' disciples take, another step backward seems to follow. Living into his role as the rock upon which Jesus will build his church, Peter displays faithful courage by stepping out of a boat onto the water when Jesus calls to him. Then realizing people don't walk on water, Peter begins sinking into a stormy sea and has to beg Jesus for assistance.[12] The disciples go to cities and towns to heal and teach, preach and proclaim God's love, returning with joyous stories of powerful transformation flowing through their acts of faithful love. Then they try to chase little children away from their busy master and want to send a hungry crowd out to the wilderness after a long day of fellowship and learning. Two steps toward transformation are quickly followed by a step or two back.

There is a part of us that wants to keep moving forward, but there is an equally strong impulse to return to the predictable—even when the predictable traps us in a beastly form and sorrowful situation. Yes, even though love can and does change the world for the better, the transformative power of love ebbs and flows. We must remain open to change and growth if love's power is to flow freely within us and through us. When Belle and Beast return from their dangerous journey in the forest, we see this ebb and flow in their budding relationship. Both begin to change, opening to one another and creating new possibilities as they do so.

HOPE OVERCOMES FEAR

As we saw above, hope is a crucial gift for Beast and the castle servants who suffer at the hands of a terrible spell. Hope is also a crucial gift to the fledgling Christian community, which suffers at the hands of religious and political authorities, even family, friends, and neighbors. But hope is a gift that can be terrifying to embrace. While it may be better to have loved and lost than to never have loved at all, can the same be said of hope? When hope is dashed, it can be devastating. Jesus' disciples see their friend and master crucified at the hands of those who then seek to destroy the followers of Jesus. If Jesus' disciples allow themselves to hope for a better day, are they only opening themselves to additional suffering? This is the same fear that holds Beast back as he and Belle form an uneasy friendship. With the petals of the enchanted rose beginning to fall, Beast has grown resigned to his doom—he will remain a beast for all time. In many ways, this resignation has put Beast on the other side of suffering. He can go no lower and simply has nothing more to fear. Is he willing to be drawn back, like Lazarus from the tomb, knowing that he will have to go through this suffering once more if Belle is not the one who will break the spell?

Like the beast of our story, the disciples spend weeks locked away from the world after Jesus' death, terrified and afraid to move forward. It takes a miracle 50 days later to break the power of their fear and fill them with hope once more. On that mystical day of Pentecost, Jesus' followers are filled with the transformative power of the Holy Spirit and find their confidence to embark on new journeys toward life-giving transformation.[13] But until that moment, they seem unclear about their path and unable to move.

Fear not only clouds our perceptions, it poisons the well of hope residing within. Like the disciples after Pentecost, as Beast tastes the sweetness of Belle's irrepressible optimism and hopeful spirit, the fear poisoning his hope slowly fades and joyful anticipation begins to emerge. We watch the gradual transformation with our own hope. Beast steps forward in hope, then retreats into his self-protective fear and then takes another step of faith by offering kindness, hospitality, and friendship to this enchanting young woman. Although Belle's journey toward kindness, hospitality, and friendship with Beast is smoother, she still puzzles over his past behavior and is somewhat alarmed over her emerging feelings. Even so, she happily engages with this new friend and his castle full of funny-looking servants. Already, Belle sees new possibilities emerging. She shows Beast how to feed the birds and pet her horse; she figures out a way they can both dine properly given his physical limitations; and she even begins sharing her joy of reading with him.

As the servants watch this transformation unfold, they are not only filled with hope, they are filled with awe, as they see this petite young woman courageously challenges the powerful beast. Even without a physical transformation, Belle grows before our very eyes. She grows braver and stronger. Her worldview expands as she engages these enchanted creatures and explores the magical castle. Her heart opens ever more widely as she explores friendship and kindness with her captor, inviting him to open his heart and his worldview in return.

Like Jesus before her, Belle nurtures transformation both within herself and others. With her welcoming openness and her loving acceptance, Belle's open-minded perspective allows her to perceive people differently, even when they are candlesticks and clocks. Her curious outlook and creative perceptions lead her to inquire about the castle community's strange dilemma and wonder about possible solutions. Late in the story, when Belle describes Beast to her father and the villagers, she paints a picture of a kind-hearted friend rather than a frightening monster. In nourishing hope and transformation, Belle's hope grows, beginning her own process of transformation in perspective and perception.

ONE TRANSFORMATION LEADS TO ANOTHER

More often than not, the one whose life is transformed is only one part of the story. This is true in the gospel stories of Jesus, in the fairytale stories of literature, and in the life stories we know from our own experience. One person's transformation opens a path for the transformation of others. We are all interconnected in the great web of life, and each strand we touch and heal affects every other strand in ways great and small. Any and all who perceive the transformation of another, or are touched by another's transformed life, cannot help but be changed.

In the gospels, particularly in the healing and acceptance stories, the transformation of one person is observed and discussed by others. Observers are always affected by what they see—sometimes they are filled with awe and wonder, sometimes with fear and confusion, and often with anger and debate. Some witness these transformations and decide to follow Jesus; some engage more fully in Jesus' teachings with questions, dialogue, and debate; some express their faith in awe and wonder at these transformative moments; still others decide such power is inherently demonic and seek to destroy Jesus' reputation. So it is with the characters of *Beauty and the Beast*. In interacting with and observing both Belle and Beast, people are affected by what they see. Mrs. Potts and Lumiere rejoice; Chip admires; Cogsworth worries; Maurice protects; the villagers fear; and Gaston attacks. Whatever our responses might be, transformation continues to reach down to communities through the ages, as people re-tell these stories, read these stories, listen to these stories, and study these stories. Such is the ripple effect of genuine transformation and the power of stories testifying to them—whether the stories are about healing the sick, raising the dead, welcoming the lost, eating with sinners, or simply inviting outcasts to rejoin society.

Friendship Contains Its Own Magic

Similarly, the communities around Belle and Beast are influenced by their burgeoning friendship. As the servants watch this surprising relationship grow, they help Beast discover ways of expressing his affection for Belle. They talk amongst themselves, wondering if Beast is capable of truly loving another and pondering whether Belle is the long-desired hope to break the spell. They dream of their own transformed lives, even as they consider Beast's potential for transformation. They remember their past with melancholy and even regret when they recall a selfish boy-prince who needed guidance. But even in this sorrowful remembrance, they dare to hope again, dreaming of a future where they are transformed back to human form.

And so, as the friendship between Belle and Beast grows, smiles and laughter throughout the castle become more frequent. Belle's inquisitive nature helps Beast explore new worlds, even within his own castle. She courageously invites him to laugh and play, dance and dine, and explore the books from his enormous library. Beast opens new worlds to Belle as well. By giving her his library and more books than she could have ever imagined, Beast offers Belle's curious mind a gift beyond price. And in the 2017 film, Beast escorts her on a magical journey to understand her early life in Paris and the origins of her father's melancholy. Beast's growing friendship and affection for Belle not only softens him, it provides him the courage to break down his fortress of self-protection and to invite her into his emotional world.

Who We Put First Changes Everything

At the end of a romantic evening of dinner and dancing, when he asks Belle if she is happy with her life in the castle, Beast is open and honest, as all true friends are. As he nervously awaits Belle's response, the animators and costume designers gift us with a beautiful Beast—a Beast who is not only handsome in his dinner attire, but in his sparkling eyes and gentle countenance. When Belle expresses her yearning to see her father, Beast shares his magical mirror, which he has kept hidden until now. Beast is prepared to offer Belle this precious object, his only window to the outside world, because he now wants what is best for Belle, not merely for himself.

Belle is the one lacking clear vision in this moment; for while she can see how much her endangered father needs her, she fails to perceive that Beast needs her every bit as much, if not more. Here, Beast is further along the journey toward transformation than Belle. She is drawn back to the familiar—to the role of a loving daughter who is responsible for the nurture and care of her father. In that familiar role, she barely glances at Beast when he encourages her to leave the castle to care for her father. Already, we can see her mind racing back through the forest to her father's side. The familiar is pulling her away. The old patterns are calling her back to the past. By automatically putting her father first, Belle fails to see that an expansive transformation is available to her—a transformation that would allow her to embrace both her father and her new companion in one expanded community of friendship and love. Returning to the familiar pattern diverts her from moving forward to new possibilities. Focusing exclusively on the familiar clouds her perception to such an extent that she does not even notice the deep sorrow in Beast's face as she races from the castle.

This is the moment that allows Beast to grow and expand. Putting Belle first, Beast has no choice but to set her free to follow her dreams and desires. Belle can no longer be his prisoner—for the love of a prisoner is limited by the imprisonment itself. In releasing Belle to return to her father, Beast releases Belle to freely and fully love whomever she chooses, never anticipating that she will use her freedom to return to him one day, much less before the rose loses its last petal.

SEEING WITH NEW EYES

Even the servants are puzzled by this strange and potentially catastrophic turn of events. Not only are they grieving their dashed hopes for Beast and themselves, they are puzzled why his love is not enough to break the spell. But this is a spell that requires the transformation of not just one, but two, and ultimately, many. Surely, Beast has earned Belle's love by now. He has loved sacrificially, given selflessly, and opened his heart to compassion and kindness—all things the young prince had failed to do. But with her new-found freedom, until Belle can learn to expand her perspective and perception in order to see with the eyes of love, she cannot achieve the transformation necessary to help Beast break the spell. She has yet to see Beast as the handsome prince he has become and truly is.

Fortunately, Gaston helps Belle's growth here. For Gaston is a man who is outwardly handsome, but inwardly a beast. Confronting him back in the village helps shift Belle's vision of her strange-looking friend in the castle. It takes the ugliness of Gaston's verbal attack on Beast for Belle to see the deeper truth about where genuine beauty resides. When Gaston sees Beast in the enchanted mirror and accuses him of being a monster, the fog clears from Belle's perception and she sees clearly that Beast is gentle and loving. In that moment, Gaston, the handsome village hero, is revealed to be the true monster in this story. Just as Belle sees this truth with clarity and conviction, Gaston's sidekick, LeFou, comes to the same realization and begins his own journey toward transformation.

As with any good story, each moment of revelation and resolution leads to greater conflict. In the moment that Belle realizes the true beauty of Beast, she and her father get locked away by Gaston while the villagers attack the castle. After Belle and Maurice escape their imprisonment, Belle races to the castle, arriving just in time to cry out for Beast's salvation. With hope rising anew and something to live for, Beast rises to fight Gaston and bests the invader only to be fatally attacked from behind. As Beast lies dying, Belle is inconsolable, unaware of the power that lies within her.

In this moment of vulnerability and deepest sorrow, the last vestiges of Belle's fortress of self-protection crumble. Lost in her grief and sorrow, Belle confesses that not only does she not want Beast to leave her, but she actually loves him. This is not the story of a frog-prince who has been trying to convince her to kiss him all along. This is the story of an enchantment that Belle had no way of fully understanding. As she declares her love for Beast, she is declaring love for someone completely other than herself. She has finally seen beyond the façade of surface appearance to the soul within. She has finally truly seen the one who has befriended her, cared for her, and fascinated her. She perceives the genuine beauty within. Regardless of outer appearances, they are a perfect match for each other. Regardless of their differences, Belle finally recognizes the affinity of their love and the depths of their relationship—a depth that extends well beyond princely stereotypes and earthly beauty.

THE MAGIC OF TRUE LOVE IS NOT FOUND IN A KISS

In this moment of true love, no kiss is needed. The deep yearning of her heart is magic enough. Stars begin to fall signaling that magic is afoot. Resurrection is at hand—a resurrection coupled with a transformation so complete that the dead beast arises as a handsome prince. Belle has saved Beast, just as Beast first saved her. Together, as they have been all along, they will now transform one another for a lifetime.

Belle is as much of a savior as Beast, and Beast is no less of a savior than Belle. There is no single rescue in this story of transformation. Together, they save each other. They save each other through their mutual love, openness, and willingness to grow and transform, even as they perceive the possibility of growth and transformation in each other. Together, their transformative love reaches out beyond themselves to their communities, and we get to watch their love transform those who are touched by their story, even we who are watching the story unfold on the screen before our eyes.

STORIES OF TRANSFORMATION INVITE US IN

Stories like the gospels and *Beauty and the Beast* do more than tell us tales of transformation, they invite us inside the stories themselves, that we too may be transformed in the hearing and the seeing. As we fall in love with an eccentric mantle clock and a frightening beast, we are encouraged to look at what passes for beauty and ugliness in new ways. We begin to question our definition of beauty when we see the unpleasant ego of the outwardly gorgeous Gaston lead him into self-absorption and narcissistic cruelty. As we see how perceptions both limit and expand the characters on screen, we are invited to perceive the world differently. Like the parables of Jesus, the story of *Beauty and the Beast* challenges us to explore our own perspectives, perceptions, attitudes, and behaviors. When do my ego and self-absorption reflect the character Gaston? How does my compassion echo Belle's purity of heart? When do I run away in fear, or turn away in doubt, as Belle and Beast do? How courageously do I pursue new ventures, and how timidly do I return to the old familiar ways? Where am I able to perceive with an open mind, and when do I close myself off and see only what I expect to see? How does this story transform my perspective and encourage me to transform my life and my world for the better?

26

As we engage this story with self-reflection, the story gains the power to transform us. As we re-tell the story and discuss its meanings, we are better equipped to discover and learn the myriad lessons it offers. Such is the case with the stories of Jesus. Although gospel literally means "good news," the Gospels according to Matthew, Mark, Luke and John only become the good news of Jesus when we listen for the life-giving messages that Jesus offers through his life and teachings. These gospel stories only become transformative when we read or listen to these stories, question the lessons, allow them to challenge us, and open ourselves to the wisdom they teach. The same holds true for Disney's fairy tale, *Beauty and the Beast*. When we engage stories of transformation with self-reflection and openness to new insights, we integrate the stories into our own stories. Only then can the transformative power of these stories truly transform our lives.

So, delve with me, if you will, into these stories. Allow them to raise your awareness as we embark on journeys of transformation. For there is wisdom to be gained as we explore the perspectives underlying our definition of beauty and our stereotypes of beasts. There is beauty to be discovered as we expand our perception of beauty to look beyond first impressions and outward appearances. There is strength to be attained by embracing a transformative and transforming community of friends and family, one that will grow with us on this journey toward ever-expanding love and fulfillment in our lives. There is power to be discovered when we embrace and extend self-giving love in our interactions with others along this journey. But most of all, there is healing to be found in realizing that *Beauty and the Beast* is more than a story of romantic love, it is a story of transformative love—a love that changes both individuals and communities. When we engage stories as imaginative as *Beauty and the Beast*, and as inspirational as the gospels, we discover a life-giving power of love that can transform the world for the better. Such is the power of story. Such is the power of love.

THE TRANSFORMATIVE POWER
OF PERSPECTIVE

AWAKEN TO A NEW PERSPECTIVE

Religious teachers, including Jesus, the Buddha, and Hindu sages, are always telling us to wake up—to be alert, alive, attentive, or aware. The title Buddha literally means "one who is awake." Henry David Thoreau wrote: "To be awake is to be alive. I have never met a man who was quite awake. How could I have looked him in the face?"[14] If we are not aware of what is truly going on around us, we go through life asleep, condemned to live enslaved to our assumptions and existing paradigms of thought and behavior. But when we awaken to the beautiful creation and yet unimagined possibilities within and around us, light shines forth and new paths are revealed. Waking up and perceiving things as they are, not as they appear to us, changes everything. A change in perspective and the related change in perception can spark new ideas, new experiences, and new possibilities.

When Belle begins to let down her walls and befriend Beast, the duo sing of discovering something new and unexpected in each other. Twice in the song "Something There," Belle sings of qualities in Beast that she hadn't noticed before. She wonders *why* she didn't see it there before. Had Beast changed or was she seeing in a new way? Had she previously closed her mind, blinding her to any new possibilities that might emerge? Perhaps she has been trapped by her negative reaction when Wardrobe suggests Beast is "not so bad when you get to know him."[15] Belle wanted nothing to do with the cruel captor who had imprisoned her father and now held her prisoner.

Did Belle fail to truly see him because she didn't really look? Surely, no one could blame her for not wanting to know this beast. But disinterest is not like Belle, who loves to dream and see the world for all of its possibilities. After all, it is her imaginative outlook that leads the townspeople to sing about how very odd and different she is. In closing off this part of herself, in limiting her perception to what she expects to see, Belle is initially unable to see beyond Beast's worst version of himself. But as they come to know each other after saving each other's lives in the forest, Belle gradually recognizes that her close-minded perspective has limited her vision, and that Beast is more than she perceived him to be. Her perspective about a beast holding innocent victims captive prevented her from looking any deeper. As she broadens her perspective and her awareness awakens to new "seeing," Belle's curiosity is further sparked and their friendship begins to grow in new and beautiful ways.

THE IMAGE OF GOD WITHIN

The path toward transformation is much smoother when we bring a creative, open-minded perspective. Perspective, or point of view, gives us a frame of reference from which we are able to perceive things around and within us. Additionally, perspective determines our attitude toward the things we perceive. The values, expectations, paradigms, and framework we bring to any encounter shapes not only what we perceive, but how we judge and interpret our perceptions.

A creative, open-minded perspective allows us to accept and embrace new information along the way and to discover new possibilities as we travel the road of life. We are not yet finished products, and as the journey of life pulls us forward to new levels of growth and being, we can develop a creative, imaginative perspective that expands our awareness and awakens us to new perceptions. Likewise, when we bring a hopeful perspective, we are better able to perceive the beauty and light that are all around us. Jesus points to this truth in his actions, sermons, and parables (teaching stories), reminding us that we are created in the image of God, and that we are the light of the world. Jesus changed the world by showing that beauty lies within each and every one of us. Only from this perspective are we able to perceive the beauty and light that are all around us.

We glimpse the ability to see God's light in Dr. Seuss's *How the Grinch Stole Christmas*.[16] When little Cindy Lou meets the beastly Grinch disguised as Santa Claus, she recognizes that he is not behaving like the Santa Claus of her family's stories. And yet, she perceives that this Santa Claus, who is hauling away her Christmas tree instead of placing presents beneath it, will respond as Santa Claus should to her question: "Why are you taking our Christmas tree?" Little Cindy Lou sees something in the Grinch that seems impossible for those of us who "know" the Grinch's "true character." It is as if she views the world, and even an ugly old Grinch, with the child-like perspective that Jesus says is required if we are to receive God's kingdom.[17] She expects Santa-like beauty and light from this stranger in her home on Christmas Eve. Perhaps in her childlike innocence, Cindy Lou is able to see beyond appearances to the magic of unseen possibilities.

Of course, she comes from a community that sees the world "like a little child," as Jesus exhorts us all to do. Unencumbered by the need to judge things based on external appearances, the Whos down in Whoville celebrate the arrival of Christmas in a town stripped bare of all decorations, gifts, and even food. The Grinch simply can't believe his ears as the Whos gather together to sing their Christmas joy. How could they celebrate without ribbons and bows, gifts and gadgets? As the Grinch's tiny heart grows exponentially in response to his changed perspective, he joyfully returns to the town with everything he has taken. The Whos' hopeful, loving perspective allows them to see beyond the Grinch's former beastly behavior, and to welcome him into their community as he discovers the goodness within himself.

Our perspective can clarify or cloud our vision. It can imprison us in previous understandings, or free us to discover new possibilities. Our perspective lays the foundation for our journeys of transformation by blocking or paving the way toward growth. When we bring a creative spirit to our journeys, we broaden our perspectives and widen the paths upon which we walk. Add a hopeful outlook, and we smooth the roads before us as we undertake our journeys toward life-giving transformation. Look for light in others along the way, and discover beauty and guiding lights we might otherwise miss.

WAS THE PRINCE TRULY A BEAST?

In *Beauty and the Beast*, perspective (and perceptions related to perspective) have a huge impact on every character in the story, beginning with a self-absorbed prince and an old beggar woman who appears at his door one dark and stormy night. In this encounter, the prince's perspective on poverty, beauty, and worth limits his ability to see beyond appearances—a limitation that will change his life forever. But the mysterious woman also brings her own perspective on heartless and spoiled people of privilege and responsibility—a perspective that ultimately determines the prince's future life.

She is reputed to have seen right into the prince's soul, determining that he was devoid of love in his heart. This determination is far more damning than one might reasonably draw from the prince's decision to simply turn away an old beggar he found repulsive. The enchantress perceives that the prince has no potential for goodness, kindness or love without a drastic change in his life. Perhaps her perception is truly magical and she is correct in her judgment. But what if her perception was based upon a limited perspective?

What if the enchantress chose instead to perceive the young prince with an eye toward his potential? What if she looked for the light within, trusting that every human is created in the divine image? What if she brought the same perspective of child-like trust that Cindy Lou brought to her encounter with the Grinch? What if she had invited his heart to grow a few more sizes in loving capacity, rather than judging him for the lack of love she perceived?

I've never been terribly enamored with the enchantress from the 1991 film for casting her spell upon the prince and his entire castle. She seems to bring a perspective that contrasts greatly with Jesus' perspective that everyone has the capacity to love and be loved. No wonder the stories of Jesus are called "gospel" stories, a word that means "good news." The perspective that every person is capable and deserving of love is good news indeed!

WHO WE ARE CREATED TO BE

Jesus' perspective builds upon the earliest lesson from Judaism's ancient creation story from Genesis 1: Humans are created in the image of God. We are all divinely created, and made to reflect the infinite love of our Source. God, our Source, creates us and crafts us for the beauty of love, not for the great void of love's absence.

Jesus sees the world from this perspective, with an eye toward the potential and loving possibilities within each and every person he encounters. Surrounded by religious leaders much like Beast's enchantress, Jesus sees the world through different eyes. Whereas his fellow leaders categorize the world in terms of unclean and clean, sinner and non-sinner, outsider and insider, Jesus refuses to accept these categories. Instead Jesus categorizes the whole world as God's world, and every person within it as a precious creature living within the loving realm of God. "The kingdom of God is within you," Jesus proclaims boldly. "Whoever welcomes one such child in my name welcomes me," he promises. Whoever sees a naked person or an old hag at the door and welcomes her welcomes God, Jesus teaches again and again. Knowing each person is created in the divine image, Jesus entered each encounter expecting to encounter the God-light within. In proclaimed statements, in parable-teachings, and in acts of hospitality and inclusion, Jesus shows us that perspective changes everything. Indeed, Jesus' expectant perspective changed more than the world of Judaism Jesus was born into; it changed the mighty Roman Empire and even the world.

NOBODY'S PERFECT

But as our story begins, there is not yet a Jesus-character in this castle. Instead, there is just a selfish prince, a self-indulgent royal class, a passive set of servants, and a judgmental enchantress who condemns a young, self-centered boy to a beastly future seemingly for a single selfish act. This poor prince! In the 1991 film, he must have been all of 10 or 11 years old, a tween or young adolescent at most. Few of us can look back on those years without regretting some selfish decision we made. Growing through adolescence, almost by necessity, precipitates some unkind behaviors and self-absorbed attitudes as young children seek self-determination and self-definition apart from the adults who shape and rule their lives.

When I was in my early 30s, I assisted at a college friend's wedding. Family tensions were high, and there were tricky moments that had to be carefully negotiated if the bride and groom were to have a joyous wedding celebration without family arguments or antics. My friend's parents had known me as a college student and still perceived me as the 20-year-old they had once known. After the lovely wedding weekend, they commented to their daughter, "We can't believe how kind Mary was to your husband's parents. She's always been so judgmental, but she was so accepting of them!" With the same hopeful, open-minded perspective they brought to their classrooms and their students each semester, they offered their hopeful, open-minded perspective to this new encounter with me. With this openness, they looked beyond their memory of me as a selfish, judgmental college student. Thank heavens her parents, both educators, had seen both the good and the bad in their students over the years and gladly looked for both in me! If not, they might have warned her away before she and I needed each other most, as we would just a few short years later. Instead, seeing the God-light shining within me, her parents encouraged my own journey toward life-giving transformation through friendship with their daughter.

Our young prince was not so lucky in his encounter with this enchantress. She brings a much narrower perspective as she views the prince to be lacking any spark of love in his heart. This enchantress judges quickly, forgoing any opportunity for second chances or forgiveness, and casts her spell upon the young prince and his castle. Jesus' open-minded perspective—a perspective that sees the God-image in all—is absent in this early part of our tale; but of course, this is a fairy tale, not a scripture lesson.

As in many fairy tales, a magical creature initiates a dramatic crisis, and perhaps this magical enchantress brings deep wisdom about the prince's need for transformation. Perhaps she came as a teacher along the lines of a Merlin to King Arthur, a wise crone sent to impart a necessary lesson to interrupt the young prince's demise into self-absorption and cruelty. In the end, the enchantress does provide an opportunity for this young prince to grow into the beautiful being God had created him to be and become. From that perspective, she brings good intentions and wise guidance to this young prince's life. But initially, she judges harshly and condemns strictly, with little acknowledgment of his potential to grow into a being of light and love.

Understanding the enchantress is particularly challenging with such limited information, as is often the case in understanding the people we encounter. Recognizing that audiences want to understand more about this mysterious enchantress, the 2017 filmmakers fill out the story of this mysterious enchantress. She becomes both the sorceress who places the prince and his castle under a terrible spell, but also the careful watcher who ultimately blesses them with journeys of life-giving transformation. Here, the prince is no boy, but a young man luxuriating in his castle at the expense of his highly taxed citizens. While he hosts a room full of French aristocrats for a decadent evening of dining and dancing, a mighty wind suddenly blows out the candles and opens the doors to reveal an old woman in need of shelter. Surely, a wise ruler or an attentive fairytale prince would have recognized that some sort of divine or mystical moment is occurring. At the very least, he would have known his obligation to offer polite hospitality, handing her to his servants for shelter and care. Instead, he rejects her, laughs at her, reviles her in front of his guests, and ignores her advice to not be deceived by appearances. Much too late, the prince recognizes she is a magical enchantress, and he is immediately transformed into a hideous beast. Such will be his fate until he learns to love and receive love in return.

Yet this 2017 enchantress seems to pull for the prince at every turn—going so far as to live among the villagers as an old spinster, directing the lightning strike that directs Maurice to the castle, and setting in motion the events that lead to Belle's ultimate arrival at the castle. This new enchantress, however we might feel about the fairness of her curse, at least offers grace to Beast as he moves toward transformation, even setting aside the condition that he must find love *before* her enchanted rose's last petal falls.

A PERSPECTIVE OF WHOLENESS

So how are we to view the enchantress? Is she a fairy godmother or an evil villain? Is she a savior or a demon? Is it possible that she is both an old lady in need of assistance and a beautiful enchantress offering blessings and lessons through her spell? Perhaps she, like the young prince, is a melding of both goodness and cruelty, light and shadow, life and death. Are we not all some combination of these things? Only from a perspective of the "both-and" nature of every living person can we see another more fully. Otherwise, we slip into a limited perspective of "either-or," defining one person as "good" and another as "bad."

Similar "either-or" attitudes frustrated Jesus. Despite a Pharisee judging a woman of ill repute unworthy of Jesus' time and attention, Jesus continues to receive her attentions. As this woman bathes Jesus' feet with her tears and her hair, Jesus reminds his followers that she has blessed and anointed him, whereas the Pharisee (the host of the dinner party) has not even bothered to offer a basin of water to wash his feet upon entering, let alone a kiss of welcome or an anointing blessing. Jesus then turns to the courageous woman who had given him all of these gifts, and offers her forgiveness and healing. He then sends her on her way, as he so often does, with the assurance that her faith has saved her and made her whole.[18] Where the Pharisee sees only a woman who has broken the rules of righteousness, sanctity, and cleanliness, Jesus sees a woman who has been created in the image of God, and who glows still with the potential for purity and cleanliness. Rather than cursing her or casting her out for her past transgressions, Jesus receives her hospitality, notices the deep remorse expressed in her tears, and extends his own hospitality in the form of forgiveness and an invitation to begin anew. Rather than judge her as either sinner or saint, Jesus heals her and makes her whole. In the same way, we are all healed and made whole in the image of our Creator.

This perspective of wholeness comes from seeing each and every human being as a divinely created child of God. In God's creation, we are all perfect. From this perspective, there is no person incapable of love nor is there a person capable only of hatred and evil. Our imperfections may create bumps along the journey of living into that perfection, but they do not prevent the divine light from living in our very being. Our inability or unwillingness to love fully, as we are called to love, simply slows down our journey of expressing perfect love for God and neighbor. Our inner beauty is always there, encouraging us to shine forth with the light of God's image.

LACK OF HOSPITALITY AND WELCOME: A TRULY BEASTLY PERSPECTIVE

Accepting the beautiful perspective that everyone is created in the image of God, and therefore capable of love, doesn't mean beastly behavior doesn't exist. In the 2017 film, we learn that the prince has been taxing people unjustly, living selfishly at their expense, and neglecting his role and responsibility as ruler. This is not just a man who hasn't fallen in love; this is a man who refuses to offer even the most basic level of compassion and hospitality to those who most need his protection and care. If only his story were an unusual one! This story stands the test of time precisely because we have all known and seen the Beasts in our world forsake journeys of transformation by rejecting the needs of others, resisting actions of love and compassion, and refusing to offer even basic hospitality to those who need it most.

Witness our world's long struggle to welcome new immigrant communities, even into countries that have been built from immigrant populations. Reflect on the long history in the United States of racial segregation—segregation legally mandated in many states for much of this country's history. Illegal as such segregation may be in 21st century North America, inhospitable divisions and unwelcoming attitudes are still reflected in neighborhoods, churches, and schools throughout the cities and towns of this diverse corner of the world. Such a lack of basic human hospitality reflects a beastly perspective of self-absorption and neglected compassion.

In French medieval culture, like first century Palestine, the basic ethic of hospitality required those with power and means to protect the widows and orphans in need of assistance and shelter. In ancient times, the extension or refusal of such hospitality was often the dividing line between life and death. Castles, forts, manors, and city walls were built to protect communities from the dangerous world outside of civilization. A fortress stood as a welcome sign of hope to people traveling from one destination to another, particularly as darkness fell or inclement weather arrived. Any weary traveler could expect to find safety and at least a modicum of welcome at the doors of a French medieval castle; for the prince and his royal household were responsible for all of their subjects, not just those who resided within the castle walls.

Scripture guides us to this same welcoming, hospitable perspective of seeing others, particularly those in need, with the eyes of love and compassion. Stories teaching the importance of hospitality are frequent throughout both the Hebrew Scriptures (Old Testament) and the gospels of the New Testament. Sadly, the stories are so numerous precisely because hospitality is so often neglected—even by communities founded upon the ethic of hospitality. A welcoming, hospitable perspective is beautiful and loving; and when lived, creates communities and strengthens relationships. When we lack this perspective, we bring our own beastly attitudes and outcomes to potentially life-giving encounters. Maintaining a welcoming and accepting perspective, in both attitude and action, creates transformative communities and strengthens our journeys toward transformation.

Regrettably, maintaining this welcoming and accepting perspective has challenged nations and peoples throughout human history. Jesus witnessed this struggle in the Roman and Jewish communities of his day. Hospitality was a common expectation among both Greeks and Romans in ancient times. Often viewed as a sacred obligation instituted by the gods, the ethic of offering hospitality to strangers held their communities together. Within Judaism, rules of hospitality were shared through the telling of ancient stories long before they were ever written down and codified into Jewish law. Jesus was well aware of this ethic, even as he knew the challenge people experienced abiding by it. Not only did Jesus' own family lack lodging on the day of his birth, they were forced to flee their homeland to escape a murderous Jewish king.[19] Raised on the stories of his faith and nurtured by scriptural decrees depicting how people were to treat one another, Jesus weaves these lessons into his own stories—stories that teach the importance of caring for strangers, neighbors, friends, family, and those in need.

Jesus speaks again and again of the importance of welcoming the stranger. In *The Good Samaritan,* perhaps the most famous of all the gospel parables, Jesus illustrates that loving one's neighbor means extending hospitality when it is most needed, regardless of how convenient it is or what we may think of our neighbor.[20] In this lesson-story, a man who was beaten during a robbery lies by the side of the road in need of help. As he lies there, a priest and a Levite pass him by—people who know and teach the religious requirement of hospitality. Astonishingly, a kind Samaritan offers assistance to the man, even though Jews and Samaritans typically despise one another. Jesus lifts the Samaritan to hero status, in contrast to the priest and Levite who pass the victim by. This story offers a two-fold lesson in hospitality. First, when someone is in trouble, we are to stop what we are doing in order to offer assistance. Second, don't be surprised when hospitality is offered, or denied, by those we least expect. A tree is judged by the fruit it bears. "By their fruit you will recognize them," Jesus advises.[21] A Samaritan, who bears good fruit, can be the kind-hearted hero of a story; and a priest and Levite, who bear bad fruit, can be the hard-hearted bystander of a story.

To understand how scandalous this parable was to Jesus' audience, some background is needed. In Jesus' community, Samaritans were the "bad" descendants of Jacob, the ones who refused to center their religious life and worship in the land of Judah—which meant they were not Jews. Even though Samaritans were descendants of the ten tribes of Israel, they followed Samaritanism, rather than Judaism—worshipping at their own holy sites, rather than at Jerusalem's holy temple, and neglecting the rules of the Pharisees who ruled Judaism in Jesus' time. Worst of all, Samaritans lent assistance to the Babylonians when they invaded Jerusalem, destroyed Solomon's Temple, and forced the people of Judah into exile in 586 BCE. Such sins just couldn't be forgiven. And so, six centuries later, Jews continued to view Samaritans as traitors and apostates, worthy of loathing and contempt. Through the power of story, Jesus shatters this unassailable perspective and prejudice, offering a radically new perspective in its place. Namely, those who care for a stranger with compassionate hospitality—regardless of heritage, label, or status—are to be praised for bringing the kingdom of God near, as they give fuel for the journey toward life-giving transformation; while those who withhold hospitality—regardless of their ethnicity, wealth, religious role, or social standing—are to be chastised for pushing the kingdom of God away, as they impede such life-giving growth.

Jesus offers a similar message in *The Parable of the Sheep and the Goats*. In this lesson-story, Jesus warns that when we fail to show hospitality to those in need, we neglect to show hospitality to God.[22] Only in welcoming the God-light in one another are we able to truly light our own path forward and light the path for others. When we neglect this calling, we limit our journey, and theirs as well. Through the power of story, Jesus teaches the importance of offering hospitality (at all times to all people) as he points out the divine connection between each and every created human being. We are all created in the image of God, and live as reflections of God's likeness. By nurturing our connection with one another, we strengthen our connection with God and with the image of God at the core of our very being. We live into that image and reflect our divine light all the more brightly when we answer the vital call to care for the least and the last. Jesus calls attention to the importance of caring for these vulnerable members in the community, because the most vulnerable are so often neglected, despite the laws of hospitality established to guide cultures both then and now.

Things were not all that different at the time our fairy tale was written in 18th century France, governed equally by its royal history and its Catholic heritage. A young prince in a French Catholic kingdom would surely have known these lessons well. He would have known that casting an old woman back out in a storm would put her in harm's way, perhaps even leading to her death. And yet, the prince of our story rejects the vulnerable woman at his door, as if her haggard appearance somehow exempts him from the expectations of a man in his position. Operating from a perspective that his likes and dislikes, his needs and personal preferences, trump the needs of others, the prince is blinded to a deeper perception of the woman. Self-absorption never leads us to manifest the most beautiful parts of ourselves. Indeed, the prince's beastly perspective leads the enchantress to change his outer appearance to reflect the repulsiveness within. While the powerful enchantress possesses no spell that can transform the prince's unloving heart, perhaps another enchanting hero one day will. As we will see in our final chapter, the seeds for the prince's transformation are actually hidden in the enchantress' spell. For the spell contains a blessing whereby a creature filled with love will drift into the prince's life and teach him how to love, even as he learns to receive love from this special being of love. And so, our story turns to a young girl living in a small French village with a

38

dreamer's mind and an optimist's loving heart—a heart big enough to save a beast.

DREAMS: A SACRED PERSPECTIVE

When our story leaves the castle to focus on a small French village, we hear Belle singing of the townsfolk as simple and quaint; we also hear the townsfolk singing of Belle as a dreamer with her head in the clouds. To the villagers, Belle is an enigma. She is a beautiful young woman dreaming her life away. To Belle, the villagers are trapped by the limits of their dreams. Their lives are predictable and small, lacking imagination. Neither sees the other in the fullness and complexity they deserve. The villagers' perspective on dreamers prevents them from perceiving how much larger life might be outside their village. And Belle's perspective on those who are happy with a simple, country life prevents her from seeing the richness of village life: a woman gathering food to feed her large family; merchants preparing their wares and opening their busy shops; a young man wandering the streets, wondering about his future marital life; a wonderful, wise mentor sharing his love of books with the beautiful young daughter of the local inventor.

When Belle's dreams lead her to sit in judgment on her neighbors, they lose their sacred power to help her see and envision a world where everything belongs. Belle is left with a naïve perspective of neighbors who are far from simple. When Gaston stirs up the townsfolk toward our story's climax, we are reminded that people who live on the edge of survival are fierce in their determination to protect themselves and their loved ones from perceived threats like Beast. We underestimate such people at our own peril.

Fortunately, Belle's dreams also bring a wide-open, broad-minded perspective to her own future story. Here, her dreams have a sacred dimension that is seen in all the world's great dreamers. Jesus is very much a man of sacred dreams himself. As a descendent of Jacob, the father of holy dreamers, how could he not be? Jacob dreamed of a stairway to heaven—a ladder connecting earth and sky with angels moving freely up and down its rungs to aid the descendants of Abraham. But Jesus' dreams were even bigger. Jesus dreamed of a stairway connecting heaven to all of God's children—even tax collectors and sinners, lepers and outcasts, Samaritans and Gentiles, children and widows. Jesus talks, dines, and shares his healing touch with these unlikely recipients of God's mercy and care, these surprising citizens of the realm of God. Jesus dreams God's dream of a world where none shall hurt or destroy one another. Dreamers carry the power of the One who bestows us with dreams.

When Belle allows the sacred dimension of her dreams to guide her perspective and perception, she sees greatness and possibility in the most unlikely of candidates: her beloved horse Philippe, who almost seems more a spiritual guide than simple companion to Belle; her father, whom she believes in and trusts unequivocally; her book-loving mentor (a sort of priest-teacher in the 2017 film, a fun spin on the loving bookseller from the 1991 film); and even the great outer world, as she sings to the heavens and the wider world of her hopes and dreams. As Belle runs across the fields and sings of her dreams and hopes for the future like Julie Andrews in *The Sound of Music*, we see the echoes of Jacob's ladder connecting her to the heavens. As she dreams her dreams, Belle almost seems aware that she is surrounded by angels of possibility, revealing songs yet to be sung, and sacred connections yet to be touched.

And so, this young dreamer brings her sacred seeing to a most amazing place of adventure—an enchanted castle, cursed by its own limiting perspectives, yet brimming with possibilities for transformation. This dreamer enters a world where a magical enchantment rules over its residents, hiding their path toward blessings and transformation. Belle is about to change the castle's fortune upon her arrival, for Belle is guided by her own blessed dreams—she is not ruled by the nightmares that haunt the castle.

CREATIVITY AND IMAGINATION: A HOLY INVENTION

Belle is more than a just a dreamer, she is blessed with the gifts of imagination and creativity. Much to the consternation of her village, Belle is a creative and imaginative inventor like her father. In almost all versions of this fairy tale, Belle loves reading and explores worlds that can only be imagined, not seen. Reading is the muse that sends Belle to faraway lands and wondrous dreams. Books unlock her mind in the mystical way of the creative arts. Disney's 2017 film expands Belle's creative nature by depicting her as an inventor in her own right—a sort of renaissance woman who draws up plans, and experiments with new possibilities, like her father before her. With an inventor's imagination and an artisan's skill, Belle cleverly constructs a device that will wash the household's laundry while she teaches a young girl to read, sharing with that child a world beyond the village's borders.

In the 1991 film, a binocular-style peephole at her front door, a mechanical woodcutter in her basement, and a waterwheel powering her home invite Belle to see the world more creatively each and every day. In the 2017 film, she is surrounded by complex music boxes, beautiful paintings, and piles of sketches exploring memories and dreams yet to come. She and her father are not limited by the routines that define the boundaries of their neighbors' lives. They share a dreamer's perspective, believing creativity, imagination, and innovation are more important than blindly following social expectations and established ways of doing things. Belle positively bursts with creative, inventive energy—an energy that pushes her to see the world in new and imaginative ways and to question the limitations of unquestioned assumptions and prejudices.

Jesus makes good use of both creativity and imagination. Through parables and lessons, Jesus explodes the unquestioned assumptions and prejudices of his day. When asked who is to blame for a man being blind since birth (the man or his father), Jesus says, "Neither."[23] By challenging their assumption that bad things don't happen to good people, and by shifting their perspective away from the need to blame someone for life's tragedies, Jesus directs his hearers' attention to the miracle he is about to perform—giving sight to this blind man and displaying God's creative, glorious, healing power. At another time, when confronted by a perspective of scarcity, Jesus challenges his audience to set aside their fear and place their trust in God's providential care. Inviting the crowd into the spaciousness of imagination, Jesus asks them to consider the birds that soar carefree upon the winds. If God provides for the birds of the air, which are sold two for a penny, how much more will God provide for them, who are worth so much more? Likewise, inviting the crowd into the freedom of a changed perspective, Jesus asks them to consider wildflowers in a field, which neither spin nor toil; yet Solomon in all his glory was not adorned with such God-given beauty.[24]

Creativity and imagination are tools that tap into the Infinite—the Source that unlocks new ways of seeing and new perspectives on the old and familiar. We see this in the stories of Jesus—stories that activate our creative and imaginative minds, inviting us to take comfort in God's protective care. We also see this in *Beauty and the Beast*—a story that leads to expanded, expansive life, based more on right loving than right living. Belle embodies creativity and imagination as she guides Beast beyond his past failings. The sacred dimension of Belle's dreams and the holy

41

Reminiscent of "Creative Power" by Hughes Mearns

invention of imagination and creativity give this story the tools it needs to be transformative—not only for Belle, Beast, and the castle, but for us as well.

CURIOSITY AND WONDER LEAD THE WAY

Belle's father Maurice is on his own creative journey as he heads off to the fair to share his beautiful creation. Finding himself lost in the woods and chased by wolves, Maurice is driven to Beast's castle, barely escaping with his life. When Maurice arrives at the dark, mysterious castle in the dead of night, his curiosity and optimistic outlook override his exhaustion and fear. I love the way the 1991 film portrays Maurice as an inquisitive explorer when he encounters the magical creatures of Beast's castle. "How does this work?" is probably a question that has guided Maurice's life since childhood. With inventors around the world, when Maurice confronts a mystery that has no clear explanation, it propels his search for answers. Mysteries invite new understanding, and as Maurice perceives his failure to grasp how such workmanship is accomplished, he begins imagining a solution. Had Beast told Maurice his story, I have no doubt Maurice would have begun drawing up blueprints for a new and improved castle experience in their enchanted circumstances. Maurice might have even been able to design a way to sustain the enchanted rose beyond Beast's 21st year, thereby granting Beast more time to learn how to love and receive love in return. I can even envision Maurice creating a matchmaking enterprise to help Beast connect with women in the outside world, for Maurice brings his creative, inquisitive, curious perspective to every facet of his life.

In the 2017 film, even when Maurice runs away from the castle in fear, he stops on the way out to courageously pick a rose for his beloved daughter—ever hopeful that he will find his way home and regale Belle with stories of a castle that is "alive." Keeping with Jeanne-Marie Leprince de Beaumont's "La Belle et le Bête" and other ancient versions of the fairy tale, a rose leads to disaster for Maurice, as it has for Beast before him. Yet the rose is more than a source and symbol of their downfall, it holds the promise of their redemption, connecting their fates, as only love and magic can. When Maurice picks a rose from Beast's garden, it sets in motion a series of events that brings salvation to Beast and the castle—as Belle saves Beast from himself, helping him learn to love and earn love in return.

42

Seeking her father, Belle arrives at the castle, bringing her dreamer-perspective with her. Even when she meets Beast, Belle is more curious than frightened. As she gazes upon this giant monster, her eyes widen with shock, but then narrow with inquisitiveness and wonder. While initially speechless in the presence of a talking candlestick and clock, Belle quickly recovers and is soon grilling Lumiere and Cogsworth for information about the castle. Curiosity drives her, and even Beast's ferocious temper is not enough to deter her from exploring the forbidden West Wing when the opportunity presents itself. As Belle meets Wardrobe, her shock again gives way to openness and acceptance of this strange being in her bedroom. And as a teapot offers dinner and plates dance before her eyes, Belle laughs and applauds, enjoying the entertainment with joy and wonder. Unlike Gaston, who perceives only dark magic and evil sorcery in objects like the enchanted mirror, Belle's curious mind never succumbs to fear of the unknown. As she wanders the dark, gloomy castle, Belle is more inquisitive about the possibilities of her strange new home than she is alarmed by the repulsive gargoyles and ugly images that surround her.

Belle recognizes that there are things yet unknown to her, mysteries yet to unfold, and lessons yet to learn. For as Shakespeare's Hamlet says to his friend Horatio: "There are more things in heaven and earth, Horatio, than are dreamt of in your philosophy."[25] Openness to the unexpected and surprising mysteries of this magical castle is a natural outgrowth of Belle's dreamer spirit. With dreams as spacious as they are imaginative, her mind is as open to new possibilities and discoveries as her spirit is free to embrace them. With her dreams and open-minded perspective to guide her, Belle is able to embrace the castle's magic and the strange creatures who are bound to it. Like Jesus before her, Belle interacts comfortably with those that appear cursed, dangerous, and frightening.

The setting of *Beauty and the Beast*, like the European middle ages, reflects a time in human history when differences were viewed with fear and suspicion. Things deemed unusual were considered ugly and strange; non-conformity to social norm was deemed dangerous, even sinful. We see these attitudes in play as the villagers sing of Belle's behavior in the film's opening song. We see these perspectives in action later in the film as Gaston sees "dark magic" in the enchanted mirror, as he plays on the villagers' fears, and as he locks up Belle and her father for being crazy and bewitched by a magical spell. The villagers' march to the castle is a typical "dark-age" response to anyone and anything perceived to be magical, witch-like, potentially threatening, or simply different.

Openness to Mystery, Wonder, and Beauty

If we are to embrace all the imaginative, creative gifts that life has to offer, we must be open to mystery, wonder, and beauty in all of their rich and wondrous forms. Openness to mystery requires a perspective that there is more to life than the tried and true habits and assumptions we accept every day without so much as a passing glance. Albert Einstein warns us to never stop questioning: "Never lose a holy curiosity."[26]

Openness to the sacred requires a perspective that we are deeply connected to divine power—whether that power is understood as God, Christ, Spirit, Allah, Buddha, Brahma, the Tao, Holy Mystery, or another name for your Higher Power. Such openness expands our perspective and invites curiosity to lead us forward to new possibilities. Unfortunately, such openness was sorely lacking in Belle's France, as it often is in our world today.

Attending a comedy night at our local Improv Theatre, many in the audience refused to believe that the comedian had really walked in cold, asked us questions, figured us out, and created a routine exposing the hilarious foibles and follies of our lives. While most of us laughed and relaxed into the evening, others resisted. Afraid of being tricked, they were convinced that here had to be "plants" in the audience. The comedian and comedy club must have sketched it all out ahead of time. With folded arms and doubting frowns, those who could not accept the genius at work in the comedian's long-practiced craft sat stone-faced throughout the performance. The rest of us simply laughed, enjoying the comedian's clever wit, quick responses, and intelligent humor.

Magicians encounter the same type of resistance and incredulity as they perform their art of illusion before our very eyes. Some of us laugh and enjoy the seemingly impossible; others grow frustrated that they can't figure out the trick. These unhappy souls insist on resisting the magic—questioning, testing, trying to part the veil of the magician's illusions. They insist that there must be trick stages, green screens, or switched props to explain the magic and illusion occurring in our presence. We all bring our own perspectives to magic shows and improvisational acts. Some of us arrive open and eager to be entertained, while some of us arrive closed off from the joy the event might bring. Is it any wonder that those who come open to being entertained, are; and those who come closed off from being entertained, aren't?

What joys might the villagers have discovered if they had embraced Belle's unusual inventions and celebrated her imaginative dreams? How differently might they have experienced the enchanted castle if they had allowed themselves to perceive the absurdity of fighting teacups and wardrobes? How much richer might their lives have been if they had been able to perceive the castle's magic as part of life's marvelous adventures, instead of being hardened against the unknown and determined to destroy what they could not understand? The 2017 film reveals how disastrous the villagers' hardness of heart would have been had they succeeded in their murderous campaign to destroy the enchanted servants. For many of these servants were forgotten friends and family of the villagers—forgotten, because the enchantress had wiped all memory of the servants from the villagers' minds. When housekeeper-turned-teapot Mrs. Potts calls out to her villager husband, Mr. Potts, he hardly notices her voice, even after sensing that there was something strangely familiar about the castle. Though the enchantress has erased their memories, it is the villagers' close-minded perspective, hardened by years of strict conformity to societal norms, that leads them to attack the castle. It is this same close-minded perspective that leads them to miss an opportunity to explore new possibilities and grow through this magical encounter. Their perspective, and its accompanying behavior, is sadly reflective of both ancient and modern times.

Contrast the villagers' "typical" behavior to Belle's atypical acceptance of her new home, its unusual inhabitants, and even her frightening new master. Belle's curiosity trumps any other stereotypes she carries with her into this magical castle. She explores, questions, and wonders at everything she finds, and refuses to allow rules or regulations to limit her curious investigations. When she informs Cogsworth and Lumiere that the castle's West Wing must be interesting or it wouldn't be forbidden, I can almost hear Jesus arguing with the Pharisees that the Sabbath was made for humanity, humanity was not made for the Sabbath.[27] By their very design, castles and their grounds are intended to serve not only the royal family, but the kingdom under the family's protection. So is the prince free to do as he wills, or does the prince bear responsibility to do as the people expect of him? Belle would have known the answer to that question: rulers exist to protect their kingdom, not the other way around. Historically, as rulers lose sight of this ethic, their kingdoms tumble and they fall from power, just as Beast's castle and kingdom are falling apart.

LET YOUR LIGHT SHINE

In Jesus' day, he could already witness the devastation of the Jewish community. He foresees the destruction of Jerusalem's temple—a physical destruction that reflects the spiritual demise of a faith community under the spell of Roman power and control. Called to be a light to the nations and the source from which God's light is to bless the rest of the world, Israel has been reduced to a shadow of her former self. The beautiful Jerusalem Temple stood atop that city, offering a glimpse of heaven. God intended that holy city to be a light upon the hill, not a cesspool of corruption hidden under political cronyism and religious abuse. Jesus calls this precious community of faith to shine forth with God's law of love, not dim its light through demands for strict observance of priestly codes. Jesus calls temple leaders and their flock to worship God in Spirit and in truth, to be a light to the nations once more—a shimmering glimmer of the presence of God in every human community.

Jesus continues to invite each and every one of us to shine the light of hope, to salt the world with the spice of life, and to proudly offer God's love for all to experience. Jesus calls all of his followers to be the "light of the world," to live in holy community as a "city on a hill," and be the "salt of the earth."[28] Each and every one of us is called to shine the light of loving hospitality. Every kingdom's castle is meant to be a beacon of hope for weary travelers and to stand as a symbol of strength to faithful peasants who work for the kingdom. The Statue of Liberty's torch in New York Harbor, the White House's glow in Washington D.C., the Taj Mahal's long reflective pool—these symbols shine the light of hope, the same light that Jesus portrays within his stories and his deeds.[29]

Like castles before and since, Beast's castle was built to offer light and hope for the whole kingdom. As prince and ruler, Beast was to portray that same light of strength, hope and hospitality to his people. In our story, the castle has long since lost that shimmer, and Beast has clearly lost sight of his duty to be a source of steadfast strength for his household and kingdom. Animators and artists for both films capture this reality as they darken the castle, only to brighten it with shimmering beauty and dazzling sunlight after the spell is lifted.

But even in the dark, dreary castle, Belle refuses to allow the castle's despair to extinguish her innate curiosity or to keep her from seeing beyond what her eyes alone can see. As Belle wanders the West Wing, she sees glimpses of the kingdom that once was. Had Beast invited her optimistic perspective and her imaginative dreaming into his life from the beginning, he would have discovered a faithful friend and a compasssionate companion—one who could guide him on new paths and open his mind to new and creative possibilities. We, who follow an infinitely creative God, can offer these same imaginative possibilities and creative options to one another. We, too, are invited to be lights upon the hills of our communities—shimmering with possibilities and revealing God's presence in our lives and in our world.

BEAUTY LIES WITHIN

Jesus teaches us that when we welcome another, we are welcoming God; and when we care for another's needs, we are caring for God. When we are able to see the light that shines within one another, we refuse to accept perspectives that seek to limit another's creative, imaginative possibilities. When we see the world from this perspective, we are able to perceive the God-light in each and every person we encounter, even those who appear to be beasts. The very act of recognizing and acknowledging the light of God within another is often enough to initiate a journey toward transformation within that person—particularly for people like Beast who no longer recognize the light within themselves. By contrast, through her innocence, her curiosity, and her openness to the world of imagination, Belle sees beauty all around. I believe her name means beauty, not just or even primarily because of her physical beauty, but because of her beautiful perspective and her beautiful outlook on the world. Long before our fairy tale was ever told, Jesus taught that beauty lies within.[30] Belle personifies this truth, for her greatest beauty comes from her inner world, not from her outward appearance.

In Disney's *Beauty and the Beast*, the disparity between inner and outer beauty is seen most clearly in Gaston, who is stunningly handsome, yet rotten to the core. In most romances and fairy tales, he would be the one to save the beautiful princess. But perspective is everything in this fairy tale, and we quickly learn that Gaston's narcissistic shallowness overshadows his outer beauty. While Beast is outwardly monstrous, we soon become enamored with the inner beauty that starts to emerge as he grows in kindness and love. Early on, we realize that a very different fairytale ending is in store for us than the ones we have seen in other Disney fairy tales.

Later in the story, Belle brings her transformed perspective—that one can look like a beast on the outside and yet be good and kind on the inside—to her neighbors, when she shows them Beast's image in the magic mirror. Transformed by the blessings this newly discover perspective has effected in her, Belle positively glows. Even Gaston can see love shimmering within her, as Belle tells the villagers that though Beast may look dangerous, he poses no threat to the village. In fact, Beast is her friend. This new and crazy perspective on beasts is a step too far for Gaston and the villagers, who choose to cling to their familiar perspective that terrifying beasts are dangerous and cruel by nature, imminently threatening to their village. The only "prudent" thing to do, therefore, is to kill the beast.

SACRED BEAUTY IS ALL AROUND

When we allow our perspective to remain entrenched in unconscious prejudices and stereotypes, as these villagers do, we lose an opportunity for growth and transformation. Conversely, when we open ourselves to sacred beauty, we open ourselves to transformative experiences that shift our perspective in holistic ways. This openness arises naturally from an open-minded perspective to the awe and wonder within all of life. When Jesus' disciples try to silence and send away children who are disturbing the adults in his presence, Jesus gathers a child into his lap and points out that children are pure of heart. Children are on this earth not just to learn, but also to teach, for we must become like children if we are to enter into God's realm.[31] Children naturally possess the receptivity that Zen Buddhism refers to as Zen mind or "beginner's mind"—experiencing all things with the enthusiasm and wonder of a child; seeing things as if for the first time. Zen mind is always aware, always that of a beginner—which makes everything new, as we allow the world to present itself to us as if for the first time. Beginner's mind requires a humility and vulnerability that is difficult for adults to achieve, but comes naturally to children. When children are filled with wonder, innate curiosity, and vivid imagination, they can easily open themselves to the mystery and magic that surrounds them every day. It's no wonder that Jesus taught that we must become childlike again if we are to perceive the Spirit that is closer to us than our very breath. Talk about a transformative perspective!

The teachings of Jesus are as true today as they were two thousand years ago: The realm of God is truly within us when we open our hearts to the open-minded perspective of possibility and the transformative power of love. Opening to sacred beauty, we discover the true beauty within one another. This open-minded perspective lays the foundation for the life-giving journey toward transformation that defines the story of *Beauty and the Beast*. Regardless of our past, regardless of our longstanding patterns of thought and behavior, and regardless of how the world judges us or how we judge ourselves, we remain beautiful beings, created in the divine image of love. We remain capable of giving and receiving love, of claiming wholeness, and of creating beautiful and spacious new beginnings, no matter where we are on the journey of life. If we allow this to guide us, we too can find a "happily ever after" by embracing life-giving perspectives on our journeys of transformation.

THE TRANSFORMATIVE POWER
OF PERCEPTION

OPENING OUR MINDS TO NEW POSSIBILITIES

As we open our minds more broadly, we are able to perceive more widely, giving transformative power to the gift of perception. As we expand our awareness with intentional mindfulness and attentiveness, we discover new perceptions, notice additional information, and experience situations differently. Alone and frightened after Beast imprisons her in the castle dungeon, Belle cannot imagine being invited to reside in a luxurious guest room. The servants-turned-household objects initially frighten her, then spark her curiosity, and eventually become her friends and companions. As her perspective on the castle moves from fear to curiosity, Belle soon realizes the castle is more enchanted than haunted, and her castle companions are more friendly than frightening.

Mindful perceptions and expansive perspectives offer us a path toward change, growth, and powerful transformation. At the same time, unexamined perceptions and blindly held perspectives have the power to imprison us in old assumptions, paradigms, and patterns of behavior. Trapped in the assumption that he will remain a beast forever, Beast succumbs to familiar patterns of temper tantrums, judgmental stereotypes, and self-absorption. Until he expands his perspective to include a hopeful outlook, Beast fails to perceive the opportunities for growth and change hidden within the spell. Despair blinds him to the wonders all around him: a castle full of books he has not read, an estate filled with servants who can provide friendship and wisdom, and a winter kingdom glistening with beauty unseen. Belle reveals these wonders to Beast, but they have been there for the discovery all along.

PERCEPTION'S DUAL ROLE

Perception plays a dual role in our lives. Perception is not only the *act* of seeing, hearing, and becoming aware of the world around us through our physical senses and mental awareness; perception is also the *evaluation* or *judgment* of this seeing, hearing, and awareness based upon our perspective. It is how we understand and interpret what we are physically and mentally perceiving. In perception's first role, Beast sees a man imposing on his castle and plucking a rose from his garden. In perception's second role, Beast judges the man to be a thief—a thief who responds to hospitality with indifference and burglary. Any transformative gifts Maurice could bring to Beast are invisible to Beast, who perceives nothing beyond an invasive thief. Similarly, in perception's first role, Belle sees her beloved father held captive in a castle tower by a frightening creature. In perception's second role, Belle knows that her father is guilty of no worse than seeking shelter from a storm (1991) or picking a rose from the castle grounds to bring a gift back to his daughter (2017). Such actions can hardly be considered criminal, much less warrant a sentence of life imprisonment! With Belle's perception of Beast as a monster now firmly established in her mind, this perception can only change if Belle is prepared to see and perceive with fresh eyes. Our religious and philosophical teachers would say that Belle is not truly awake, for she has closed her mind to the possibility that Beast can be more than he appears. Until she reawakens her mind with openness to new possibilities, she is unable to look beyond appearances and see the prince within the beast.

Perception and perspective have the power to fuel a journey toward transformation or to halt this journey in its tracks. Optimism invites hope and encouragement, whereas pessimism invites fear and fatalism. A clear-eyed perception coupled with an open-mind invites imagination, creativity, and new learning; while a clouded perception coupled with a closed mind discourages new possibilities.

This contrast in perception is evident throughout the story of *Beauty and the Beast*. Even as some characters personify one more strongly than another, each character brings varying levels of perception and contrasting perspectives into their individual experiences, as most people do. On my best days, I am open to new ideas; I am filled with new possibilities and dreams; and I am aware of God's infinitely creative power. At my very best, like the Queen of Hearts in *Alice in Wonderland*, "I've believed as many as six impossible things before breakfast."[32] On other days, old paradigms kick in and I bring a more limiting perspective, failing to perceive the miraculous possibilities inviting me onward. Where we place our focus, and how we interpret what we perceive impacts how we behave, react, and interact with the world around us.

Perception Determines Our Direction

Beauty and the Beast opens with not just a limited perspective, but also a mistaken perception. A woman appears at the castle's door, seeking shelter for the night. A young prince opens the door to meet this woman. To the prince, the woman appears to be old and ugly, reminiscent of evil hags so prominent in fairy tales he has heard as a child. He perceives nothing of worth in this woman's visit.

In the 2017 film, when the prince refuses the woman's request for lodging, his haughty, self-absorbed guests approve of his dismissal of the old woman, deeming the prince's actions both justified and wise. Yet, it's hard to imagine that the prince fails to perceive the woman's need for assistance, poor and helpless as she seems. Wise rulers, in both fairy tales and in real life, heed the pleas for help and hospitality from those in need. But our young prince is not a wise ruler—he is a foolish young man who rejects the obligations of duty and honor, a young man who has shut his heart, a young man in need of transformation.

How did the prince come to perceive this old woman as being beneath his concern? Did her physical appearance shroud the lessons of chivalry he certainly learned growing up? Even when the old woman warns him not to be deceived by what his eyes show him, the prince still sees only poverty and ugliness before him. Even with signs that this woman is more than she appears and that magical forces might be at work—the candelabras blowing out, the foreboding silence that fills the castle as the castle doors fly open at her arrival—the prince cannot shift his perception of the old woman. Focusing on her outward appearance, he turns her away, demanding she leave without shelter or assistance. The prince's callousness becomes a missed opportunity to open his heart, but it also begins a journey he would never have imagined, much less asked for—a journey easily sidetracked by a mistaken perception.

It Is Only with the Heart that One Can See Rightly

Jesus spends much time teaching his followers to see with the eyes of their hearts, because he knows that perception helps determine the path we follow. Jesus teaches his followers to see beneath the surface, to look beyond the letter of the law and the rules of their faith, to discover the spirit of God's teachings. Jesus notices people, notices their possibilities, and notices when those possibilities are being squelched; then he creates opportunities for people to transform those possibilities into realities. Jesus sees with enlightened eyes and invites others to do the same, offering hope in the face of despair. He opens up worlds of opportunity where none seemed to exist before, living this prayer of the writer of Ephesians: "With wisdom and revelation, may your heart's eyes be enlightened so you discover the hope to which you are called."[33]

Perhaps this is why the prince has no hope after the spell. He clearly lacks the wisdom and revelation to have the eyes of his heart enlightened. He cannot see beyond appearances and refuses to heed any advice to look more deeply. Is the prince's perception based on selfishness and cruelty because of a loveless heart, as the enchantress diagnosed? Or, is he only able to see with his physical eyes because the eyes of his heart are not enlightened—a condition so dire that the prince cannot even see the beauty and worth in the rose the enchantress offers?

"It is only with the heart that one can see rightly," writes Antoine Saint-Exupéry in *The Little Prince*, "what is essential is invisible to the eye."[34] The young prince of *Beauty and the Beast* is blind to this heart-centered seeing. Without the ability to see with the eyes of love, the prince misses the truth before him. He perceives no beauty, no possibility, and no purpose to this old woman's visit. In so doing, he misses an opportunity to serve, an opportunity to offer compassion, and an opportunity to grow. In these mistaken perceptions and missed opportunities, the young prince cannot embrace the gifts, blessings, and transformation this powerful enchantress offered. All too soon, his mistaken perception creates a haunting new reality for everyone in the castle.

When the "old woman" reveals herself as a beautiful enchantress, she is prepared to teach the selfish prince a harsh life lesson. As her outward appearance fades away, the prince sees the depth of his mistake. Might the wondrous lady before him have been a potential princess to share his life, or a fairy godmother with gifts and blessings to share? This enchantress is not only blessed with physical beauty, she is endowed with magical abilities that might have bestowed bounty and riches to his kingdom. But now it is too late. The beautiful enchantress cannot help this ugly-hearted prince until he can perceive the world with the eyes of his heart enlightened. Perceiving that there is no love in the young prince's heart, the enchantress transforms his outer form to reflect the beast within.

But the enchantress doesn't stop there. She not only turns the prince into a beast, she turns everyone in the castle into enchanted objects, and the castle itself into a place of darkness and foreboding. We have no explanation for the reach of the enchantress' spell. Was she herself blinded by a limited perspective and mistaken perception of this young man? Could not this ugly old woman have found a kinder, gentler, and more loving way to guide the prince's steps toward transformation? We will never know. All we know for sure is that our spoiled prince perceives nothing more than a worthless old woman at his castle door, and our veiled enchantress perceives nothing more than a monstrous young man sneering before her.

WHEN JUDGMENT BECOMES JUDGMENTAL

From this very first scene, we see the ease in which perception can become judgmental. The prince's judgmental perception of the poor old women is echoed later in the film by Gaston, when he warns Belle that she does not want to end up like the "spinster" Agathe. The enchantress seems judgmental of the young prince as well—perhaps stereotyping him as one of those unfeeling royals, who fail to care for those they are charged to serve and protect. Regardless of her intentions, the enchantress' perception rests on a limited perspective that the prince can be defined as either beastly or manly. Perceiving the former, the enchantress judges that there is "no love in his heart" and acts accordingly.

The question then is whether the enchantress' judgment is sound or is simply judgmental. From one perspective, her judgment seems reasonable. When judging a ruler such as a prince, we expect certain ethics and behaviors. The young prince should have offered hospitality. Rulers should put their country's interests ahead of their own. When leaders neglect these leadership ethics, we wring our hands in concern and rightly object to their behaviors. But do we also conclude that the leader is "bad" or "evil" or "a jerk"? This perception, or judgment, is far too common in our world today.

While judging leaders in this way may seem justified, offering such judgment quickly becomes judgmental. Perspectives that see others as only "good" or "bad" lead easily to judgmental perceptions. We may miss the potential to see goodness and beauty. Expecting to see the worst in others, we begin to see the worst that we expect to see. The enchantress saw a bad ruler; the prince saw a worthless old woman.

Such judgmental perceptions are not limited to labeling powerful leaders; they also lead us to label and stereotype the least powerful or most unfamiliar people in our world. People may assume persons of a different ethnicity are dangerous or dirty or lazy. People may label persons of a different political or religious persuasion as evil or ignorant.

54

People may perceive young people or the elderly to be burdens on society. People may assume a homeless person deserves his situation, or an erotic dancer must really love or hate her work. Often, the people who are most in need of protection and compassion are the people judged most harshly in our world today.

On the other hand, when we look for unseen beauty and unrealized potential in ourselves and in others, we discover a new way of seeing. We begin to perceive possibilities we might have missed otherwise. Relationships we might never have formed suddenly become life-changing, as we learn to see with the eyes of our hearts. New paths forward are revealed as we look about with wide-eyed wonder. We can begin to imagine dozens of impossible things, even before breakfast—but only when we open fully, and perceive clearly.

PERCEPTION CHANGES EVERYTHING

Having watched the harrowing drama of *Beauty and the Beast* unfold before our eyes, we are left with the task of examining our own perceptions. How do we perceive the magic of the enchantress? Is it merely a spell intended to correct the prince and lead him down a path toward transformation, or is it a curse intended to punish the prince along with his entire household? Is this beautiful enchantress a canny guide to lead the prince to his own salvation, or is she a destroyer of dreams, someone who brings ugliness and grief to the young prince's life? Looking at the 1991 film, we might perceive the enchantress as a bit of an evil hag, despite her transformation into a physical beauty. Who is this judging, curse-riddled magician, who seems destined to bring the prince and his entire household to disaster? Despite her outward appearance, it is not beauty that the enchantress brings, but a curse of beastly proportions.

But is this negative perception of the enchantress fair? Is it even warranted? Narrators, magicians, and soothsayers come and go in literature, particularly in fairy tales—often with knowledge that readers and viewers are not privy to. Initially, it seems the enchantress brings only misery. But if we change our perspective, might we not perceive her as a beautiful prophet of power and possibility? Can she be offering both curse and blessing? Perhaps it is our ignorance of what it means to be this enchantress that prevents us from perceiving her in a positive light. For the enchantress seems to know that without her spell, the prince will remain imprisoned by his cold heart forever. Perhaps she even knows

55

that if the prince's servants are not enchanted right along with him, he will not be able to receive their help when the opportunity arises to see with the eyes of his heart enlightened. As we watch her character unfold in the 2017 film, we gain a more charitable perception. This enchantress even gains my admiration—for she sees the prince's growth in love so clearly that she sets aside the terms of the spell and offers grace and rebirth even after the last rose petal falls.

When the prince is reborn and is transformed into his fully human self, the community is reclaimed and fullness of life returns to the castle. Memories return, families are restored, and all celebrate the transformation of this formerly horrible prince into a man worthy of their love and respect. This is a beautiful scene filled with forgiveness and grace—a scene portending love and hope for the future. But it is a scene made possible through a transformation of perception by almost everyone in the story.

THE POWER OF PERCEIVING POSSIBILITIES

Consider how quickly the Whos change their perception of the Grinch when he returns to Whoville with their stolen Christmas gifts. The Whos do not let the Grinch's past behavior prejudice their perception of current realities. When the reformed Grinch appears in town, the Whos recognize that the Grinch who is returning their Christmas gifts is not the same Grinch as the one who stole their gifts to begin with. They perceive someone new, someone with a larger heart. Just as they know that Christmas has arrived, despite missing their Christmas decorations, they can see that a new friend has arrived, despite his monstrous appearance and bags full of stolen booty. This is clear seeing indeed!

Clarity of vision is often strongest in community, particularly when we are surrounded by people who perceive possibilities and look for the best in us. The entire Who community appears to see beyond appearances, explaining Cindy Lou's optimistic outlook on a strange-looking Santa even as he strips her home of decorations and gifts. In most biblical stories, it takes a community (or at least another person) to clear up confusion and create such clear seeing. Certainly in Beast's case, it took an entire castle community to open his heart to Belle's friendship and to begin seeing possibilities that escaped him before.

In the biblical story of Esther, Esther's foster-father Mordecai begs her to risk death and ask her Persian king to spare the Hebrew people. "Who knows" Mordecai asks, "whether you were not born for such a time as this?" Reflecting on his words, Esther begins to see herself as more than just another queen in the king's harem; she sees herself as a powerful, creative child of God, reflecting the divine light within her. As her perspective changes, she perceives new possibilities for her life. Esther discovers her boldness, her power, and her ability to initiate change. In so doing, she creates an unexpectedly empowering new path for herself and for her people.

With the same sense of purpose and possibility, Belle walks courageously through the dark and enchanted castle. Who knows whether she too was not born for such a time as this? Even Beast sees this truth at some level; his castle servants certainly do, as do we who watch these marvelous films. Ah, such is the power of a good fairy tale! We are all whisked into Belle's hopeful perspective and imaginative dreaming. Surely Belle's purpose is to help Beast break the spell by learning to give and receive love. Surely Belle will be the one to save the castle from the twisted fate it has known all these long years. We know she can do it. Positive and powerful, she is the one. Belle has convinced us, even before she has convinced herself—for Belle has the ability to sing her dreams into being. We know she will discover and fulfill her purpose, even before she understands what her purpose is. For Belle has shared her hopes and dreams with us, and we are now part of her community— a community that will walk this path with her, wherever it may lead.

THE STRANGE PATH TO REDEMPTION

As our confidence in Belle expands and our hope grows, tragedy strikes again. Even as we explore the castle with Belle and celebrate her courage, we tremble in fear as Beast lashes out in anger. Belle leaves the castle on the very night of her arrival, departing out of frustration and anger at Beast's cruel temper. Later in our story, she will leave again, this time out of love and concern for her father. On her first night in the castle, we want Belle to stay, and yet we admire her courage to flee. Is there any hope in her departure? Is there any chance her departure might yet prove transformative for Beast, turning the enchantress' spell from curse to blessing?

Even as we lament Beast's loss, we applaud Belle's refusal to be a victim. We know that she cannot save Beast from himself—he must embark on his own journey toward transformation. Beast must not only learn to control his temper, he must learn to open his heart to love and to become vulnerable to the growth love brings in its wake. As long as

Beast resists such growth, Belle's presence in the castle will be a pleasant diversion from his fate, but nothing more.

As Belle rides away, our minds are invited to ponder possibilities. Will Beast learn from her departure? Will he calm his temper and extend a bit of kindness to his servants? Will he beg Belle to return once she saves her father? With his expensive education, Beast could resort to the age-old tradition of composing a sonnet, or he could find selfless courage and show some genuine contrition by writing a letter of apology. In traditional versions of the fairy tale, Beast sends secret gifts with Belle, blessing her family with goods and necessities to satisfy both their wants and their desires. But Disney's films offer a different opportunity for Beast to grow toward the loving transformation he needs.

Unexpectedly, Belle is no longer escaping to freedom, but facing lethal danger in the forest. The wolves that had once chased her father to the castle are now preventing her escape. As they snap and snarl, Beast surprises us all by emerging from the dark wood to save Belle. A vicious fight ensues, leaving Beast gravely wounded, but not before besting the wolves and sending them yelping into the night. Assured of safe passage, Belle almost leaves Beast to die. But her inner beauty shines forth, as she remembers the proper response to such a sacrificial gift. Filled with gratitude and compassion, Belle returns to the castle, helping Beast along the way, prepared to nurse him back to health.

GRATITUDE OPENS DOORS TO EXPANDED PERCEPTIONS

As Belle returns to the castle with the injured Beast, there is little assurance that any good will come of it. Beast has saved Belle's life. She in turn has saved his. But even after returning to the castle to care for him, an argument erupts over who's to blame for the mishap. In the midst of their argument over Belle's painful ministrations and Beast's ferocious temper, something unexpected happens. Belle offers a word of gratitude: "Thank you for saving my life." These six simple words shift everything. Beast remembers his proper royal manners and accepts her gratitude with a quiet "You're welcome." In the 2017 film, they quietly settle into a peaceful coexistence of care giving, healing, and contemplation, saving their words of gratitude for another time. Later, Beast expresses his gratitude that she didn't leave him to be the wolves' next meal. In this act of genuine thankfulness, we see the prince Beast was meant to be.

Gratitude possesses a magic all its own. Suddenly, even the servants see that something new has begun. Beyond hope and expectation, Beast remembers what it is to be a prince; and Belle perceives a kindness in Beast that doesn't fit with his terrifying appearance and temper—a kindness that saved her life. In their changed perceptions of each other, achieved through heroic action and simple exchanges of gratitude, new possibilities emerge for each of them. Everyone but Chip, the boy-teacup who is too young to understand such things, can see something present that wasn't there before. Hope kindles in hearts throughout the castle—hope that gratitude will lead to understanding, understanding will lead to affection, affection will lead to love, and love will lead to the transformation of the prince and the castle community.

As the enchanted rose wilts and loses its petals, the possibility of love begins to bloom and grow for Belle and Beast. This beautiful step forward—the step that shifts perceptions and opens us to dream of new possibilities—begins with the miraculous gift of gratitude. Remembering to give thanks resets our perceptions and centers our thoughts on blessings rather than complaints. It opens us to new horizons. While Jesus does not speak frequently *about* the power of gratitude, his life and ministry are a testament to the power of giving thanks in everything he does: giving thanks for the opportunity to show God's glory before raising Lazarus from the dead; offering thanks for the mysterious way God reveals truth to the innocent and pure of heart while hiding it from those the world considers wise; giving thanks before turning a few loaves and fish into a feast for thousands; and returning thanks before offering the bread of life and the cup of salvation at the last Passover meal he shares with his disciples.[35]

It is often said that people of faith are the only Bible most folks will ever read. If this is true, acts of love and gratitude carry far more power to transform people's lives than preaching does. While Belle gets a little preachy with Beast after he scares her into running away, expressing gratitude brings her back to center and directs her actions thereafter. Rather than criticizing Beast when he takes his many blessings for granted—an unsurpassed library, gorgeous castle grounds, servants who truly care for him—Belle models gratitude in almost everything she does. At times, she offers gratitude with a simple "thank you;" at other times, Belle expresses gratitude through her sense of wonder and awe.

TRANSFORMATIVE DREAMS: THIS OR SOMETHING BETTER

As Belle begins to recognize her expanding perspective and changing perception, she sings of her new-found wisdom, even as she admits to her growing lack of certainty. Contemplating the new and alarming feelings that have expanded her perception of Beast, Belle continues to ponder her circumstances and her role at the castle. She yearns for freedom, yet she is also strangely drawn to this larger world in which she finds herself. Where will these conflicting feelings and thoughts take her? How can she be a hero in this tragic tale if she is a prisoner? If she leaves the castle and returns to her quiet village, will she continue to grow and make her dreams come true, or will she shrink back to fit her sleepy little village?

As Belle's perception of her plight changes, her perception of her former dreams changes as well. Each new question she asks, each new song she sings, each new poem she reads, each new conversation she has with Beast, and each new adventure they share, brings a shift in awareness and a shift of perspective. And each shift of perspective affects her dreams. Realizing that her dreams must be allowed to grow and change, she begins to dream: "This or something even better."

Within the castle, Belle lives in a world that is wider, more wonderful, and more terrible than any she has known before. In the 2017 film, when Beast invites Belle to use a magical book to travel anywhere in the world her heart desires, Belle returns to her roots—the artist's loft in Paris where she was born, the location of her mother's illness and death, the place her father could not bring himself to speak of. Discovering the gruesome truth that her mother had died of the plague, Belle asks Beast to take her "home"—not to the village where she has spent almost her entire life, but to the castle where she has spent but a few days. It is not lost on Beast that Belle calls the castle "home," and it begins to pain him that he once referred to her as nothing more than the daughter of a thief.

Belle's perceptions and perspectives are changing so fast it makes her head spin. She has always dreamed of so much more than the provincial life of her little village, but those dreams never included being held prisoner in a castle suffering under a dark enchantment. She should be miserable, and yet she is not. Even her perception of her prison has changed as she brings her hope-filled dreams to her relationship with Beast and to her place in the castle. Just as Beast begins to perceive himself as truly human, despite his appearance, Belle begins to perceive herself as truly free, despite her pledge to remain as Beast's prisoner.

Perception is a powerful ally on the journey toward transformation. Simply seeing ourselves in our transformed state moves us forward on the path of transformation. I've often wondered if Jesus was such a gifted healer because he saw people as already well and whole. His seeing helped them see this truth for themselves. As Beast and Belle begin to perceive themselves in this new and beautiful way, their perception of each other deepens, and they are better able to help each other live into their dreams. As we watch their friendship grow and mature, we see how fully Belle can save Beast, and how fully Beast can save Belle in return. They are both in need of transformation, for they are both imprisoned by more than castle walls and an enchantress' spell. As they begin to fall in love in spite of themselves, we yearn to celebrate their happily ever after. We long to watch the magical transformative power of love and beauty grow within and between them. We hope to see outward appearances melt away, as inward resistance crumbles. We dream of watching their dreams come true. But how is it possible that this will happen?

THE TRANSFORMATIVE POWER OF STORY

The film is cleverly crafted to pull us into the heart of the story—to root for the castle community as they cheer Beast on toward higher levels of transformation, and as they cajole Belle to persevere in her role as hero and savior. From this point forward in the film, we feel a part of the community. We are all in. We laugh, we cry, we hope, we despair, we applaud, we groan, we sigh, we wring our hands—but most of all, we anticipate and long for a happy ending. Like it or not, we are now inside the journey of *"Beauty and the Beast."*

Likewise, when we read the gospel stories and allow ourselves to fall in love with the characters, no matter how flawed they may be, we get inside the stories and the stories get inside us. We begin walking with Jesus, bumbling along with his disciples, laughing and crying with the crowds. Stories offer different glimpses into the world for others to see. When we share stories with others, we invite them inside worlds with perspectives that are different from their own. We can help others change their perspective and perception, just as Jesus did, through the power of story. Telling others to change their perspective is almost universally greeted with resistance and pushback, but telling these same people a story allows them to try a new perspective on for size as they enter the world of the story. Likewise, when we hear the stories of others and open our minds to the perspectives inside those stories, we invite in new possibilities with new perceptions.

Certainly, Belle's imaginative perspective paves the way for a transformed perception. Entering Beast's story as openly and willingly as she enters the stories of his odd-looking servants, Belle discovers a new friend and recognizes that there is something more than just a beast in this master of the castle. And as her perception grows and expands to embrace this new friendship, Belle is suddenly able to relate to a beast as if he were a human friend, just as she does with his servants, be they clocks, wardrobes, teapots, or candlesticks.

As we explore stories with others, we grow and expand together. Jesus teaches that when two or three of us are gathered together, God is in our midst, for surely a story is being told. Whether in a church, synagogue, mosque, temple, ashram, sacred hoop, or simply with a committed group of friends, our sacred stories help us offer mutual love and support. They help us cheer one another on in our quest for transformation in mind, body and spirit. Communal stories of hope help us through times of trial and tribulation. Communal stories of joy help us celebrate with one another during moments of laughter and mirth. Shared stories of peace and justice help us work to make our world a better place and to build the very realm of God in our midst. As we share our sacred stories and allow these stories to move us to action, our creative God joins us and works within and through us. Great Spirit flows in our minds, hearts, conversations, and endeavors. The Source of mystery and life invites us into a freer, fuller, more expansive view of the world—all through the power of shared story.

As our stories grow, so too do our ideas, perspectives, and shared viewpoints. Our minds open to new perceptions, and our imaginations flow in new directions. We begin to connect with dreams and innovations that are lying deep within—dreams that are held down by our logical, practical minds, but are now set free. In sacred stories, the impossible is always possible, and the improbable seems laughingly easy. Communal stories bind us together and set us free. Such is the change a good story can make.

JUST A LITTLE CHANGE

From their first encounter, Belle and Beast bring very different perceptions and perspectives to the world they encounter. When they meet initially, Beast refuses to allow Belle to say goodbye to her imprisoned father, thinking such courtesy is not owed a man who has trespassed in his castle or stolen a rose from the gardens. When Belle protests the injustice of imprisoning a man for picking a flower, Beast objects to her characterization, arguing that if refusing a rose can condemn him to eternal damnation, stealing a rose certainly justifies imprisoning a thief forever. Turning his own logic against him, Belle defends her request to kiss her father goodbye, saying: "Forever can spare a minute."[36] By questioning his rationale from a different point of view, Belle changes Beast's perspective ever so slightly. And in so doing, Beast adjusts his perception of her, if only by a little. And so begins his slow but steady journey toward transformation—a transformation that begins for him with a small change of perspective and perception. This small shift in perception upsets Beast's entrenched perspective and initiates further changes in perception—changes that are necessary if he is to break the spell and be transformed back to human form.

Belle's dreamer perspective spurs her curiosity about Beast, his castle, his servants, and this mysterious spell they are all enduring. As she contemplates Beast's childhood and the paths that led to this moment, she realizes her knowledge has expanded and her perceptions have changed. Some of her innocent perspective fades away in the light of this new understanding, but a wiser openness emerges that allows her to see more clearly, befriend her beast-friend more fully, and interact more freely, despite her imprisonment.

As Belle brings more of her dreamer's perspective and curious perceptions to this new friendship, Beast's perspective and perceptions begin to change as well. Growing more open and honest with Belle, Beast allows himself to be more vulnerable as he shares his stories; he even allows himself to be a bit happier as he injects his dry sense of humor and strong opinions into their conversations, debates, and playful interactions. By the time they are strolling along the path of his winter garden, Beast begins to see his own estate and grounds with a new set of eyes, as if he is "seeing it for the first time." As Beast glances around in wide-eyed wonder, we are reminded of Belle's wide-eyed exploration of both her hometown and her new castle. Belle's dreamer perspective is changing Beast's perspective, opening him to his own dreams and creative expression. Beast listens attentively to the stories and poems Belle loves so dearly, as if he is hearing them for the first time. Beast's hardened perspective, frozen like the grounds of his enchanted castle, begins melting away—slowly warming in the presence of Belle's natural wonderment, just as the earth warms with the first kiss of the sun.

We see this most clearly in their relationship to the library. Beast's enormous library, filled with more books than one could possibly imagine or read in a lifetime, brings a light to Belle's eyes—a light that brightens Beast's perception of this marvel as well. Books he has taken for granted as a young man are miraculous gifts to Belle, whose local book collection was limited at best. As she begins reading the books in this magnificent library with unbridled joy, Beast begins reading and appreciating the stories and poetry of his childhood. These are the types of shared experiences that change our lives. Just as Belle's deep love for the books of his library helped Beast discover his own love of reading, our appreciation for the things we love can help another discover or expand their own appreciation.

This is the gift that life-giving friendships bring. When we are with friends who are grateful, our own gratitude flows more easily. When we surround ourselves with others who are open-minded, creative, and who expect the best in us, our perspective expands to encompass their perspective. And when we see the best in others, when we look for the light and life they bring into the world, we act as mirrors, reflecting the truth of their lives back to them—helping them see the beauty that lies within. When we forge relationships with people who see and reflect the truth within our lives, we blossom and grow like flowers after a spring rain. And just as the rose responds to the light and warmth of the morning sun, we respond to the warmth of loving friends who see the light and beauty of our lives. Never has a fairy tale expressed this wisdom as clearly and brightly as the story of *Beauty and the Beast*.

A NEW VANTAGE POINT

Even as Belle and Beast tentatively explore their burgeoning friendship, its life-giving nature expands Beast's perspective and perception of himself and the world around him. From this new vantage point, Beast begins to hope and even dream of new possibilities—perhaps Belle is the one. Surely she is more than the mere daughter of a thief. She is worthy of love—worthy of being courted and wooed by the prince of the castle. The beast who had once scorned such a possibility is receding into the shadows as he begins to give of himself more freely and generously. Their friendship grows, as they play in the pristine snow, feed brave little birds, and pet the hesitant Philippe; their love blossoms as they explore the imaginative world of books, and even when they compromise over proper dining etiquette. Beast begins to perceive himself differently, acting and responding in a loving and princely manner. The prince who is taking the beast's place realizes that he is the one who needs to earn her love, just as the enchantress has foreseen.

However hesitantly, Beast embraces this hopeful spirit as he prepares a ball to celebrate their budding friendship. Recognizing the effect Belle's beautiful attitude has had in the castle and in his life, Beast wants to honor her with a night of romantic music and royal dancing. Now that he can perceive the beauty of this new friendship, Beast can also perceive the beauty within his own magical castle. Unsure whether Belle will ever truly see beyond his beastly outward appearance to perceive an inner beauty he can scarcely see in himself, Beast hopes for the best as he prepares for this special evening.

In what we would expect to be the climax of this great love story, our unlikely pair arrive in gorgeous tuxedo and gown for an evening of candle lit dining, romantic violin music tableside, and a magical dance in the castle's magnificent ball room. After days of strolling through the castle gardens, relaxing over a good book, and laughing over their contrasting table manners, these two young friends dance across the ballroom floor and into our hearts. We can see love blooming before our eyes. Something new is developing and a happy ending seems imminent—not only possible, but likely. For just as Belle and Beast see each other differently, we too see a handsome prince in this giant, but regal, beast floating around the dance floor with the beautiful Belle of the ball. Beast is becoming human again where it counts the most—his frozen heart is melting away to embrace warmth, kindness and friendship. Love is already transforming more than their perspectives and perceptions, it is transforming their very selves. As Belle and Beast become the people they see in each other, they live the truth Shakespeare expresses in *A Midsummer Night's Dream:*

Things base and vile, holding no quantity,
Love can transpose to form and dignity.
Love looks not with the eyes, but with the mind.[37]

PERCEIVING LOVE

Pete Townshend's poetic lyrics point to this powerful, awakening gift of love, when he sings "Let my love open the door."[38] As Belle begins to see Beast with loving eyes, she is filled with an even larger sense of wonder. As Beast begins to perceive Belle with his own eyes of love, he rediscovers the power of hope.

As they relax on the balcony at the end of their romantic evening, Beast discovers another aspect of the transformative power of love: the ability to put someone else first. When Belle expresses her desire to see her father again, Beast presents her with the gift of the magic mirror he once hid from her. This seemingly large gift of trust pales in comparison to the next gift he offers. When Belle sees her father in danger, Beast releases her from their agreement, sending her away from the castle as a free woman to aid her father. Beast knows this will result in his demise, for the castle is crumbling, he is aging, and the final rose petal is about to fall. Without Belle, he cannot break the spell. Nevertheless, love has made these considerations mute. Love has transformed him into the prince he was born to become—a kingly being with such heart and virtue he is willing to sacrifice his own life to save the life of his beloved's father. The formerly self-absorbed prince is willing to sacrifice his own hopes and dreams for a better future, in order for Belle to return home to care for this beloved old man in her life. This is a transformed perspective indeed.

Love changes everything, even our story's ending. What might have led to true love's kiss and Beast's transformation into a handsome prince turns into a sacrificial act that seems to doom the physical transformation he has sought for so long. And yet, this turn of events is the very step both Belle and Beast must take if love is to truly transform Beast into a creature directed by love, and Belle into a loving hero who can see with the eyes of her heart enlightened. In the end, this detour will not only guide their steps, but transform their lives.

THE POWER OF LOVE

Sometimes, a change in circumstances or scenery is necessary to expand our perspective. Even our open-minded hero Belle, with her loving heart and wide-eyed optimism, needs to expand her perspective in order to love Beast fully and thus become the savior of our story. As she departs the castle to find her father, Belle sees Beast as a loving being, a kind-hearted friend, and a special gift. But she still sees Beast as a beast, not as a human being like her. Only after leaving the castle does she give voice to her expanding perspective and changing perception.

After returning to the village, Belle tries to describe Beast's newly emerging inner beauty to her father, who can't believe his ears. She tries to explain his kindness and gentleness to Gaston and her village neighbors, who look at her like she's concussed. As Belle looks at Beast through the magic mirror, eyes aglow with emotion, even Gaston notices she might be falling in love with this mysterious creature. Belle's perspective is expanding toward a very different perception of her former captor, and her heart is opening to the possibility that he might just turn out to be the love of her life. Surely, such a realization must have been shocking, revealing how very far her perception of Beast has changed and how her perspective of who would make a good life companion has expanded exponentially. When Belle rushes back to the castle, she is frantic to protect Beast from Gaston; but it is only when she sees Beast dying before her that she can finally give voice to the truth of her heart: "I love you." The idea of losing him forever has unlocked the final resistance to love's full bloom and to Belle's own transformation. From the silence of love's inexhaustible reservoir, Belle speaks the words rising in her heart: "I love you."

Henri Nouwen writes: "Out of eternal silence . . . God spoke the land, the sea, and the sky. God spoke the sun, the moon, and the stars. God spoke plants, birds, fish, animals wild and tame. Finally, God spoke man and woman. . . . A word that bears fruit is a word that emerges from the silence and returns to it."[39] When Belle breaks the silence in her heart, her words of love bear fruit and break the enchantment holding Beast and the castle under its spell. As the words fall from her lips, Beast is resurrected from the dead and his beastly form transforms to reveal a handsome prince. Belle has learned to love with the eyes of her heart enlightened. She has learned to see beyond appearances, to give and receive love in spite of spells and mysteries that get in the way, and to love with an all-embracing and accepting love.

Instinctively, we know that this is the powerful lesson of their love story: To love unconditionally is to expand our perceptions and embrace even those who seem to be "other;" it is to love beyond the limits of previous perspectives. We know that Belle has learned to love Beast just as he is, regardless of whether he ever appears "human again." When we visit Disneyland or Disney World, we don't see Belle and the prince together for character appearances. We see Belle and Beast. Watching them dance or sing or sign autographs, we know that this is how they looked when they discovered true love. Disney's marketing team is wise enough to portray the prince before his return to human form—for we grow to love Beast just as Belle does, and we hardly recognize the man standing before Belle when the spell is broken. Every time we see artwork of Belle and Beast, or watch them waltzing before us, Belle and her handsome prince are transformed in our minds by the love we know that they share in this classic tale.

Perhaps this is what Jesus means in the Beatitudes when he says the pure in heart are blessed, for they shall see God.[40] Loving with a pure heart allows us to see deeply into the loving truth of everyone we encounter. When Belle perceives Beast with a pure heart, his beastly form doesn't matter. He is a beautiful being, a child of God just like she is. Of course he can be her true love. Pure hearts do not need a handsome prince or a perfect princess to experience the love that lasts a lifetime. Pure hearts perceive each human being as a beautiful child of God, and strive to love others as fellow children of God, despite appearances.

In Greek, there are three types of love: *agape*, *eros*, and *phileo*. *Beauty and the Beast* is more than a story of *eros*, or physical love; it is a story of *phileo*, or loving friendship. As Belle and Beast discover the love of friendship, *phileo*, they are able to move, however haltingly, toward *eros*. But *eros* is not the love that ultimately transforms the pair; that is *agape*, or unconditional love—a self-giving love that does not count the cost, a love that does not expect anything in return. *Agape* is the type of love Jesus speaks of in the Gospel of John when he says: "Love one another." *Agape* is also the type of love Paul writes of in his advice to the Corinthians, and the type of love John speaks of in his epistles, which are often referred to as "love letters."[41] Love is the heart of the gospel, just as it is the heart of this fairy tale.

As Belle and Beast open their hearts to love in all its glorious forms—the love of friendship, the love of attraction and affection, and the love of self-giving—their perceptions of each other expand and they move toward transformation. Unlike stories like *Cinderella* and *Sleeping Beauty*, *Beauty and the Beast* is more than just a story of two young people who find romantic love together. They discover and learn much from one another, and find the love of friendship and self-sacrifice before they ever discover romantic love. Together, they create amazing beauty before they ever marry and create a family of their own. For, this is the story of transformative love—a love that changes perspectives, changes perceptions, changes lives, and changes the world. Now, that is truly a story that can help people live happily ever after.

THE TRANSFORMATIVE POWER
OF SELF-GIVING LOVE

Greater love has no one than this:
to lay down one's life for one's friends.[42]

Love is a big deal in the gospels. Love is a big deal in fairy tales. Ask a Sunday School teacher, a romance writer, or even the Beatles, "What's the primary point of life?" and the answer will undoubtedly be, "Love." But in many fairy tales, love is reduced to romantic attraction: Love brings two young people together; love conquers evil; love helps a prince and princess find one another and live happily ever after. If it's all romance all the time, we're only talking about *eros*. This is not the case in *Beauty and the Beast*, which introduces a more complex and self-giving journey of love.

Our journey begins when Belle chooses to take her father's place as Beast's prisoner. The journey continues when Beast makes an unexpected gift of self-sacrifice to save Belle's life in a forest full of wolves. Even after Belle breaks her word never to run away, Beast saves his prisoner at great personal cost, almost dying in process. Belle, in turn, saves Beast, returns to her castle imprisonment, and nurtures her wounded captor back to health. Immersed in these adventures, we realize this is not your typical Disney fairy tale and this is not your typical Disney couple. Before they are even friends, these two characters give of themselves generously, even sacrificially.

Jesus speaks often of loving and self-giving generosity. He calls love the "greatest commandment," teaching us to love God and to love our neighbor as ourselves. Through the parables he shares and through his own example of self-giving love, Jesus offers a vision of what it means to put others' needs ahead of our own: healing when it's against the rules or when it causes trouble; interacting with outcasts, and dining with sinners, even when it leads to condemnation; refusing to abide by unjust laws or corrupt government demands; and speaking against injustices, even when it threatens our very lives. Self-giving love lies at the heart of the gospel and guides Christians to not only admire the teachings of Jesus, but to follow them as well.

Self-giving love pervades the story of *Beauty and the Beast*, creating deeper paths toward transformation through love and self-sacrifice. First, we see Belle's generous nature toward her father, as she sacrifices her freedom to protect him. As the story progresses, we see her love grow and expand beyond her family to include this strange beast who has imprisoned her. Eventually, we see Beast's generous nature grow and expand through his friendship will Belle. As Beast learns to love, we see him discover his "muchness," to borrow a phrase from *Alice in Wonderland*. In the previous chapter, we saw that the love in friendship, *phileo*, has transformative power of its own. But when it leads to *agape*, the self-giving love at the heart of our story, anything is possible.

The theme of self-giving love runs deep and strong in this beautiful story, with characters expressing their compassion and care in a variety of ways. And by the end of the film, Belle, Beast, and many others have given of themselves selflessly, creating a transformational ending unlike any other fairy tale we know and love.

THE HERO'S JOURNEY: A JOURNEY OF SERVICE

When Belle leaves home to search for her missing father, we realize she is not a typical Disney princess. She leaves without hesitation, doggedly pursuing him through dangerous forests to a dark and enchanted castle. Like Jesus traveling through Galilee, Belle is on the hero's journey as she searches for her father and finds an enchanted castle. Often, the hero's journey toward transformation starts out in a similar way, with a similar choice. We are called away from hearth and home to a new adventure, not for adventure's sake, but as a response to a crisis, a need, or a deep sense of purpose. Belle and Jesus personify a beautiful version of the hero's journey: the journey to serve, the journey to help another, and the journey to serve a higher purpose.

This journey emerges from the yearning to serve another, to seek the lost, and to save the one who is in danger. Belle's guiding value is one of service and self-giving love for a father who has loved and nurtured her over the years. Not every hero's journey in life or literature begins this way, but it is the reason that Belle begins her journey. The self-giving nature of such a journey adds its own spiritual power and imaginative strength. Self-giving in our journeys to understand and embrace our highest selves transforms us in beautiful ways. Powered by self-giving love, Belle and Jesus embark on journeys that will transform more than just themselves, they will inspire and nourish the transformation of others along the way as well.

The hero's journey is at its strongest when others benefit from our journeys, even as we benefit from theirs. As we embrace our new perspectives, expanding perceptions, and opportunities for self-giving on the journey, we move faster and faster toward the life-giving transformation we seek.

LOVE IS BEAUTIFUL TO BEHOLD

And so, Belle embarks upon just such a journey. Over the river and through the woods, to an enchanted castle she goes. Upon discovering her imprisoned father in a dark, dank castle tower, suffering in his sickness, Belle vows to help him escape. When Beast arrives, Belle has options beyond self-sacrifice. Belle could have fought, perhaps discovering a miraculous power to best even a huge beast. She could have played the trickster, a common trope in fairy tales like this one, out-thinking and out-maneuvering the cruel beast to escape the treacherous castle. But Belle chooses self-sacrifice, taking her father's place as Beast's prisoner, and setting up the primary theme of our story. While cleverness, courage, trickery, or even magic might have freed her father, love alone, particularly self-giving love, has the power to transform lives.

Envision the moment of Belle's first gift of self-giving love. In the dark prison tower, even as Belle kneels in fear and trembling to be near her father's prison door, she looks up at the villainous monster who refuses to release her father, and offers herself in his place: "Wait! Take me instead."[43] Even the hard-hearted beast before her is softened for just a moment at this surprising gesture—one she has offered humbly, quietly, perhaps even regretfully. Beast asks incredulously: "You would take his place?" Beast, who had been a selfish adolescent, can hardly fathom the selfless love Belle displays in this moment. Has he never known a loving family? Has the love he once knew been corrupted by a tragedy in his past? Or has his own heartless attitude prevented him from receiving the love that was offered? At this point, all we know is that he is surprised to witness this beautiful act of self-giving love.

Imagine what a sad childhood Beast must have endured to find a selfless act between parent and child so shocking. Generous and self-giving acts of service are common in families—but apparently not for the young prince. His reaction is a vivid reminder that self-giving love can effect powerful change when witnessed by others, particularly those who have not known such love.

Many years ago, during a long overnight flight with our young son—a son who struggles with motion sickness and excruciating stomach cramps—my husband and I sat awake, trying not to move as our small child settled across our laps and sought the relief that only sleep can bring. As we endured fatigue and stiffness in an effort to spare our son pain, we were doing what thousands of other parents have done before us, and thousands more will do in the years ahead: sacrificing personal comfort and the need for sleep in order to care for this small person in our care. It didn't feel like much of a sacrifice at the time. After all, we had just enjoyed a wondrous vacation together on Maui, and we knew we would return home in a few hours to a warm, comfortable bed, where we could rest and recover from our long flight. But as we departed that flight several hours later, an older woman touched me on the shoulder and said, "Your son is a very lucky little boy. Your love for him is beautiful."

UNEXPECTED MOMENTS

Beast may not have offered such articulate words to Belle, but his surprise marks how deeply he notices the young woman's deep, abiding love for her father. Even when he scorns her for being a fool in the 2017 film, he is puzzled and curious about this strange woman's decision. It seems unthinkable, but could she bring a perspective he needs? What is this illogical choice of sacrificing one's young life in exchange for a parent's final years of life? In this brief, transformative interchange, we see "just a little change," as Mrs. Potts will later sing.[44] But it begins right here in this initial encounter—just a tiny movement, expressed in Beast's cleverly animated face, an indication that possibilities are already emerging from this first moment of self-giving love. Only a person like Belle—someone capable of such love—could break through Beast's defenses and break the spell. Belle's sacrificial love will save more than her beloved father, it will save one in even greater need of saving.

As Belle considers Beast's demand for a lifetime of imprisonment, she takes a closer look at this "horrible, hideous beast," as Maurice calls him. Even as she gazes upon his monstrous form, Belle holds true, unwavering in her resolve to save her father. Beast, on the other hand,

72

hardens his own resolve to be beastly and cruel. As he demands that Belle remain with him forever, her courage rises to meet this sacrificial demand. "You have my word," she promises, looking boldly up into his eyes.[45] This exchange is indelibly printed on my mind—an exchange between a small young woman and a beastly monster, an exchange that shows Belle to be a giant in spirit and Beast to be a small wounded animal. Belle's sacrificial love rises to heroic proportions and sets the stage for a story filled with unexpected gifts of expansive love.

Opportunities for self-giving and sacrificial love often arise in surprise moments like this one. We notice a homeless man buying a cup of coffee for his friend, and are moved to buy him a meal as our heart includes him in our circle of compassion. The self-absorbed mother senses the powerful tug of love while seeing her baby suffer from illness, and becomes the self-giving mom while caring for her beloved child. The busy entrepreneur puts his ventures on hold to care for an aging parent when he suddenly realizes that the next six months are all they have left together.

Many years ago, a beloved church leader received a much-needed kidney donation, not from one of his closest family members, but from a church member who had simply grown to know him through the church's prayer list. The donor was not one of the "saints" of the church, but a driven political leader who focused mostly on his work, fitting in family and church responsibilities when he could. Seeing the love his church friends had for the man, and hearing their genuine pleas to God for help, he simply had to help. After quietly signing up for the donation match program, receiving word that he was a perfect fit for the needed kidney, and going into surgery to donate his kidney, this politician was suddenly the one requesting prayer. To this day, I'm not sure if his spouse even knew he had been tested to see if he was a potential match. Certainly, the recipient and his church family were surprised by this sacrificial offer—an offer that became a miraculous gift of life for a dying man. But the politician knew, and his life was forever transformed by the experience. To this day, he claims that donating his kidney was the best gift he's ever given; and he names that moment as a highlight of his life, clarifying his purpose both as a man and as a leader.

THE GREATEST LOVE: POWERFUL AND EMPOWERING

Jesus says that there is no greater love than to lay down one's life for one's friends.[46] Through the centuries, this ethic has bridged cultural and religious divides, and inspired countless people to sacrifice on behalf of others, even when it meant risking their very lives. As he talks to his disciples about the love he has shared with them, Jesus prepares them to offer this same love to one another, to God, and to God's world. Although Jesus speaks of love throughout the gospels, emphasizing the Great Commandment to love God and neighbor, his call to sacrificial love is unique to the Gospel of John. Written much later than the other gospels, at a time when Christians were enduring martyrdom and torture, John's gospel surely provided a crucial message of encouragement to offer sacrificial love, even in the face of death.

In *Beauty and the Beast*, when Belle offers herself in exchange for her father's release, she is the first character to display this type of self-giving love. But she is not the last. As the story progresses, other characters follow suit, yet none with Belle's level of vulnerability. Belle's character runs the risk of being seen as a sacrificial lamb, or even as a victim of domestic abuse. But the story turns in a different way, particularly in the Disney versions. Belle grows stronger and more assertive with each encounter with Beast. His tirades and temper do not result in increased violence on his part or increased submission on hers—she simply ignores and rejects his attempts to control her. Belle claims her right of self-determination proudly. Despite her imprisonment, she will no more acquiesce to having dinner with him than she will tolerate his vicious temper. These are not the actions of a victim, but an equal.

In some versions of Christianity, self-sacrifice and suffering are glorified in ways that oppress and imprison women, children, and the vulnerable. Jesus' own suffering and self-sacrifice are lifted as examples to be followed and as justifications for bad behavior. During traditional wedding ceremonies, wives are told to be submissive to their husbands, but how many husbands are told to cherish their wives? Both admonitions come from the same passage of scripture.[47] Battered women are told to sacrifice their dreams and their desires for their families, as Christ sacrificed himself for them. This is a cruel misuse of scripture that perpetuates abuse in ways completely antithetical to Jesus' teaching. In both Jesus and Belle, we see courageous self-definition and power as they step forward to give of themselves lovingly and even sacrificially. These are not powerless victims, suffering their fates by submitting to powers that have overwhelmed them. These are courageous and powerful leaders who transform the world with the power of self-giving love, freely offered.

Jesus teaches us to give of ourselves freely and selflessly, going so far as to say that we are to love our enemies and pray for those who persecute us. But he does not teach these lessons in order to glorify suffering or condone violence and abuse. Rather, he invites us to love courageously with confidence and power, and to sacrifice selflessly in order to save and protect the most vulnerable among us. Belle knows that her father is too old and weak to survive life in the castle tower and so does everything in her power to protect this man who has loved and protected her.

When Belle sacrificially takes her father's place in the castle, she is neither acquiescing to abuse nor giving up on herself. Out of her own sense of power and strength, Belle offers herself to protect a vulnerable, aging parent. In giving of herself so courageously, her sense of power and strength expands, helping her overcome her fears of this strange new place and this strange master of the castle. We see this as Belle travels the castle freely, stubbornly refusing to dine with her captor, curiously exploring the forbidden West Wing, and bravely escaping Beast's outburst of temper. When Belle and Beast eventually become friends, their friendship is egalitarian, arising out of mutual gifts of self-giving and selfless acts. So mutual is their growing respect and appreciation for each other, it's easy to forget that Belle remains a prisoner in the castle, until she reminds Beast in the 2017 film that one can't truly be happy unless one is free.

SEEDS OF TRANSFORMATION

For Beast's transformation to occur, this cannot be the story of a prisoner forgiving her captor and falling in love with her abuser. This must be a story of love given and received fully and freely. Before friendship can grow between Belle and Beast, they must meet on more equal footing. The servants seem to know this intuitively, encouraging Beast to bring Belle into the guest wing of the castle and to provide her the extravagant hospitality afforded to a proper castle guest. Cogsworth encourages Beast to invite Belle to dinner, which throws a wrench into things when Belle refuses. Morphing from gracious host back to beastly captor in the blink of an eye, Beast commands her to dine with him. When Belle continues to refuse, Beast storms away, ordering his servants to deny her food unless she eats with him. Yet even in his anger, Beast's own curiosity is awakened, leading him to look into his magic mirror for another glimpse of this enigmatic woman. As he notices her despair, we begin to glimpse a possibility of compassion or empathy, perhaps even a tiny step toward the transformation he so desperately desires.

Indeed, we see that the seeds of transformation are being awakened, as this unexpected guest brings a magic of her own to Beast's enchanted castle—a castle falling into decay as the rose wilts. Belle's purity of heart, her sacrificial love for her father, her insatiable curiosity, and her joy light up the darkness and gloom of the castle and everyone within it. Despite Beast's strict orders to the contrary, Lumiere and Mrs. Potts host a glorious meal for their new-found guest, and even the self-protective Cogsworth hosts a castle tour for this mysterious young woman. Predictably, Belle's inquisitive nature leads her to sneak away from the formal tour and explore the castle on her own.

But when Belle wanders into the forbidden West Wing, Beast flies into a rage as Belle reaches toward the dying rose, carefully protected under glass. While this outburst may have resulted from a sense of vulnerability, it is clearly not new behavior for him. "You must control your temper!" is a mantra Beast's servants repeat to him throughout the film. His tantrums and beast-like behavior have long been the prince's deepest curse—a curse that led the enchantress to place a spell on him in the first place. No one should be confused that Beast's monstrous form is the cause of his bad behavior, it simply reflects the person within.

New to the castle, Belle is not accustomed to his violent outbursts, and finds them intolerable. Unwilling to imagine a life where she has to endure Beast's bad behavior, Belle breaks her promise and flees the castle. This is an interesting decision for our would-be hero. After all, Belle has given Beast her word that she will stay—and heroes are typically true to their word. But Belle answers to a higher ethic—an ethic demanding the respect she deserves. If her captor's behavior renders him incapable of showing her such respect, Belle feels no compunction to abide by their agreement.

A parallel with Jesus comes to mind in his refusal to abide by the rules of the Pharisees—deeming such rules unworthy of his obedience. Jesus sees all too well the beastly behavior that results from prioritizing "righteous" actions and strict adherence to "religious" rules above the call to perform acts of justice, mercy, and compassion. And so Jesus heals on the Sabbath, dines with sinners, and touches those who are "unclean," even when it means he will be labeled a false prophet by the religious establishment. Likewise, Belle refuses to tolerate Beast's bad behavior, fleeing from her captor, his castle, and her promise to stay with him forever.

Transforming a Beast into a Hero

From the first moment of our story, we can see that the prince acts badly. This is not the type of prince we are accustomed to seeing in fairy tales. We expect a prince who is kind and loving, a prince who is gentle and chivalrous with his princess, a prince who is the very definition of a hero. Instead, our prince is a beast, inside and out. Our prince even seems to be the "bad guy" of our story. What is going on here?

Unbeknownst to Belle, Beast follows her into the woods. Why does Beast follow her? He is clearly not beholden to the rules of chivalry, and he doesn't seem intent on capturing her and bringing her back. So, why is Beast following her? Is he feeling some regret for his childish selfishness and uncontrolled temper? Is he finally fulfilling his proper duty, as master of the castle, to protect his kingdom and all of its citizens? Or is he drawn to something ineffable inside her—a quality that is elusive, yet compelling; a quality that cannot be held captive? Whatever the reason, Beast follows Belle into the woods, finding her under attack by a vicious pack of wolves.

Knowing he is outnumbered and endangered by the wolves, Beast charges into the fray, offering his first gift of self-sacrifice in our story—perhaps his first gift of self-sacrifice ever. Beast manages to frighten the pack away, but not without a terrible cost to himself. Falling wounded to the ground, Beast will certainly die if the wolves return, as they surely will. Even if the wolves don't return, he is likely to succumb to the freezing cold of a wood trapped in perpetual winter. Why would Beast risk his life to save the daughter of a thief, as he sees her, and a breaker of her word? This is not the behavior of a villain. This is the behavior of someone capable of greatness. And so Beast's heroic journey toward reclaiming his humanity begins—a journey fueled and strengthened by a transformative act of self-sacrifice.

But how does this happen? How does a self-absorbed, self-pitying, and self-centered prince-turned-beast become a hero? His unexpected moment of heroism hints that this is no ordinary fairy tale. Transformation is afoot, and more surprises are surely in store. In true gospel fashion, the one who appears to be bad, outcast, sinful or evil, is redeemable, even capable of greatness. Inside each of us is a hero, ready to emerge. Beast's transformation into a heroic savior, protecting his prisoner even as she seeks to escape him, is a bit like Zacchaeus' transformation in the Gospel of Luke.[48] Somehow, in meeting Belle, Beast connects with his higher self. Likewise, in meeting Jesus, the corrupt tax collector Zacchaeus connects with his higher self. Drawn to this traveling rabbi who radiates power from within, Zacchaeus climbs a sycamore tree to get a closer look.

When I see Beast surreptitiously follow Belle into the woods, I think of Zacchaeus hiding in the tree, hoping to see Jesus. Both are drawn to people who radiate the powerful light of love from within—a light that is foreign and enigmatic to them. Hidden in shadow, Beast wants one last look at this mysterious person who would sacrifice herself and her freedom for the sake of her father.

DRAWN TO THE LIGHT

People filled with light and love are fascinating beings. When we are at our best, we are drawn to them; but when we are at our worst, we are repelled by them. Beast's struggle to embrace the sacrificial light and love within Belle reflects our own struggle to embrace the sacrificial light and love within ourselves and others. People of light and love seem to hold up a mirror that reveals our shadow side—the beast that lurks within, the selfish child that never really grew up, the self-pitying adult that would rather nurse old wounds than let go of the past. Sometimes we envy those who radiate light and love. Other times we question their purity of heart, or doubt the sincerity of their sacrificial acts of beauty and light. But here's a secret: People filled with light and love also have a shadow side. And even when we feed the wolf within that would destroy us, the wolf that would save us remains inside, yearning to be fed by light and love. Even though it remains a beast of the wild, it is this wolf of beauty and light that draws us to people like Jesus and Belle. It is this wolf that sparks our curiosity and leads us to look with fascination at creatures of light and love—even when we feel the need to hide, like Zacchaeus and Beast before us.

When we come to realize that our shadow side does not define us, we are drawn ever more closely to people of light and love. We are freed to allow their loving example to seep into our very souls. We are freed to connect with our own yearning to love more fully, and to shine more brightly. We are freed to choose the path of life-giving transformation. Beast discovers this new freedom, as he observes this mysteriously beautiful woman, surrounded by vicious wolves and in need of protection and assistance. Rather than protecting his own interests, Beast makes a different choice, a choice that will nourish the seeds of the very transformation he so desperately needs.

Zacchaeus, a man who had used his position to enrich himself at others' expense, has a similar experience in his encounter with Jesus. Before Jesus has a chance to call Zacchaeus to repentance, or pray for his redemption, or even teach him a parable on generosity and financial ethics, Zacchaeus repents of his former life—offering to repay anyone he has wronged, and pledging to share his ill-gotten wealth with the community. Such radical transformation is unusual and miraculous, even in the gospels, and it often happens within those we least expect. At the foot of the cross, an unnamed Roman centurion who participated in Jesus' crucifixion exclaims: "Surely this man was the son of God!"[49]

When we become aware of the divine light that surrounds us every day, and when we let it illuminate the divine light within ourselves, something magical happens—we embark on a path of inner transformation that is beautiful to behold. And as we embrace this new path, higher and higher levels of transformation are revealed. This is the transformative magic that pervades *Beauty and the Beast*—a magic most clearly witnessed in the relationship between Belle and Beast.

STRANGE MAGIC

I suspect that Beast is fascinated by Belle's goodness, even as it mystifies and perhaps repels him. This is a behavior he has not seen in a very long time, if ever. The puzzled turn of his countenance seems to ask: "What is this strange behavior of one who would sacrifice her young life for her father's aged life?" Perhaps Beast senses a mystical light emanating from her. I am reminded of a line at the end of *Harry Potter and the Sorcerer's Stone*. Professor Quirrell, who is sharing his soul with the evil Lord Voldemort, cannot bear to touch Harry—a boy who was conceived in love and whose skin carries the magical protection of his mother's sacrificial love. When trying to strangle Harry, Quirrell's hands begin to burn as he encounters the mysteriously powerful protection of love in Harry's skin. Looking at his maimed hands, Quirrell cries out in wonder and dismay: "What is this magic?!"[50] When Beast calls Belle a fool for sacrificing herself in the 2017 film, I can almost hear Beast's puzzled mind cry out: "What is this magic?!"

Love is indeed a magically powerful force. Mysterious and strange, love remains elusive to those who are selfish and uncaring. It is an even greater puzzle to those who are immersed in evil and cruelty. How can one give so freely, even sacrificially, of oneself? Beast deems Belle a fool for taking her father's place. This selfless act is an enigma to the prince who has lived only for himself and his selfish desires.

Jesus was just as much of an enigma to many in his day. On trial for his life, Jesus stands before Pontius Pilate, refusing to defend himself or even submit to Pilate's authority. Knowing that he has the power to crucify Jesus or set him free, Pilate asks: "Aren't you going to answer?" as Jesus remains silent. "See how many things they are accusing you of."[51] A cruel man comfortable with wielding violence to keep the population in check, Pilate cannot figure out this mysterious man of love and light. He seems frustrated and intrigued by Jesus in equal measure. Even as Pilate condemns Jesus to death, he refuses to accept responsibility, according to the Gospel of Matthew: "I am innocent of this man's blood. . . . It is your responsibility."[52]

It is difficult to square this account with historical record, for Pilate crucified thousands of Israelites and was ultimately removed by Rome for being excessively brutal. At the same time, the account bears the ring of truth when I think of other beastly people who have been both repelled by, and drawn to, people of great love and light. Was there something about this Jesus that made a man as cruel as Pilate stop and wonder if he was missing something? Although we will never know what transpired in Pilate's chambers, the gospels depict a compelling account of his unexpected yearning for innocence in the presence of true innocence. Pilate was not the first or the last to be drawn to the mystical presence of Jesus—a man of both Love and Light who has inspired followers all around the world.

LIGHT CALLS TO THE DARKNESS

Light calls to darkness, rising with the moon and sun each day. Love calls to hate, pulling forth the love that has created us since the dawn of time. Hope calls to fear, shining in the darkness of despair. Had Pilate heeded this call, he would have released Jesus, despite the crowds' cry to crucify him. But the familiar pull of power and cruelty wins the day, sending Jesus to his death, despite Pilate's misgivings in the presence of this unusual man. In his curious questioning and confused response to Jesus, I see the spark of the man Pilate was created to be—a man capable of reflecting the divine image within, rather than the beast he chose to feed and become.

80

We are all created in the divine image, created in the force of light and goodness. This is not a fairy tale. Nor is this simply George Lucas's depiction of "the force" in *Star Wars*. This is the creation story of the human community—the sacred and mythic tale of earth's formation, spoken in the first two chapters of Genesis. This is the gospel that John proclaims when he speaks of the Word and the Light that shines in the darkness. This is the story of the Spirit of God that was in the beginning and continues with us here and now in the person and spirit of Jesus, the Christ.[53] This is the gospel that testifies to the light shining in the darkness—a light that no darkness can overcome.

As creatures created in the very light that has shined since the dawn of time, we are naturally drawn to the light. If we choose to dwell in darkness, or wander in caves and tunnels, we may lose sight of this light, but the light remains. Even if we try to extinguish the light that shines within us, a spark remains that can never go out. Even if we feed the beast of fear and anger and hatred, and even if our eyes grow dim to the light within and without, still the Light remains—calling us and drawing us forth to the Source of that light, which is our true home.

No wonder Beast is drawn to follow Belle. She is a reminder of the being he once was, and truly is. She shines the light that calls him back to the Light from which he came. She is the personification of the very love the enchantress warned him was missing in his heart. As a person of love and light, Belle reminds Beast that he too is a creature of love and light. He simply has lost his way. As light and darkness flow through our lives, we choose where to focus our attention. When we follow the light, the path to life-giving transformation grows clearer, and the path becomes smoother. But when we surround ourselves in the shadows of fear and doubt, anger and despair, the light may fade from view. In *Song for Someone*, U2's Bono and the Edge say it this way, "If there is a light you can't always see…. and there is a light, don't let it go out."[54]

At some level, Beast knows that if he turns to the light and notices its beauty and power, he will open a door to self-awareness, revealing that he too is a being of light, with the same potential for self-giving love. And so, Beast follows Belle into that dark wood as she tries to escape, knowing somehow that there are lessons to be learned—lessons of self-giving and transformative love, lessons that may help him break the enchantress' spell.

In his pursuit of Belle, Beast glimpses this truth as he discovers a bit of light within himself. When she is endangered, Beast jumps into the fray and risks his very life to save hers—not to bring her back to captivity, but simply to save her life. In this act, Beast is the one sacrificing himself for another as he falls wounded to the ground on the road to impending death in the cold and dangerous wood.

LIGHT WINS

As the wolves run away and Beast collapses, Belle prepares to ride away from the woods and reclaim her freedom. But as she glances back at Beast, the light and love that make her who she is hold her back. In that moment, Belle develops an empathy and compassion for a being she hardly knows and certainly dislikes. Her ability to befriend and love Beast gradually begins to grow. After all, Belle is not God; she is simply human. Belle may have a great reservoir of love and may be capable of heroism, but she remains in her humanness, with all the potential for growth and maturation that entails.

Here in the dark wood, Belle makes the life-changing decision to sacrifice her freedom for the sake of her captor. Returning to the castle, she bravely nurses his wounds, as Beast growls and protests with each painful treatment. As Belle attends to Beast with the same care she would have offered her father, the love and light within her glows more brightly. As Belle learns to love someone she dislikes and hardly knows, her compassion and love deepen, revealing the truth of Jesus' words that loving our enemies matters. Loving those who love us is easy; it is loving those who mistreat us that defines *agape*, the love of God. When we love our "enemies," the very act of loving opens us to higher levels of transformation and self-giving love—leading us into a brighter world.

Light wins when we embrace the light, and watch the shadows flee before it. Light wins for Belle, who would have simply traded one form of captivity in the castle for another form of captivity in her provincial town. And light wins for Beast, who would have died in that dark wood. Without Beast's intervention, Belle might have shuttered the light within her; and without Belle's decision to take him back to the castle, Beast would have remained imprisoned by the darkness shrouding the light within. But light overcomes darkness for both of them. As Belle tends to Beast's wounds, the seeds of gratitude and friendship begin to grow. Light wins as Beast's ability to love blooms, revealing his better self, his human self. Light wins as this odd pair embark on an unexpected friendship.

Eros Is Not Enough

And so a deeper path is forged, and a journey toward higher transformation begins. As Beast opens his heart to tenderness and compassion, love stirs and gradually changes his life, revealing the path to reclaim his full humanity. A sweet inner story begins, and the audience anticipates the fairytale ending that is surely just around the corner. Belle comes down to dine, clothed in beautiful royal gowns. Beast dresses up and starts acting like a gentleman. They laugh, they play, and their friendship grows. Like those early images of Jesus' teaching and healing, we like this part of the story. We hum along as Belle, Beast, and the servants sing of this surprising turn of events in "Something There." We laugh at snowball fights, cross our fingers and hope for the best. As love emerges, the spell will surely soon be broken. Watching love's bloom stirs us, romances us, and pulls us to rejoice in love.

Watching love flower is a beautiful gift, as we see the transformative power in loving and learning to love. But we have only scratched the surface of love's power. The deeper message comes from heeding the call of self-giving love and sacrificial service for the good of others. This call to self-sacrifice is a unique aspect of *Beauty and the Beast*—an aspect that doesn't fit the mold of other Disney fairytale love stories: Girl meets boy; girl and boy fall in love; an impediment to their love arises and is overcome; girl and boy share true love's kiss and live happily ever after. In these fairytale love stories, true love's kiss seals their journey and ushers in their happily ever after. Not so in *Beauty and the Beast*, for this is not actually a story about *eros*, or romantic love. In *Beauty and the Beast*, romantic love is a by-product of *agape*, a much richer, sacrificial love—a love that leads to personal and communal transformation.

Having Belle and Beast fall romantically in love may seem like the key to breaking the spell—the servant's certainly think so—but the power of mutually self-giving love will be needed on this journey toward transformation. Mrs. Potts has it right when she explains that the spell cannot be broken simply by Beast finally learning to love—Belle has to love him in return. Belle cannot decide to love Beast any more than Beast can decide to love her. Both must be transformed by love itself. Perhaps Mrs. Potts is the wise crone who knows that true love (*agape*) is much more than just a romantic dance and a gentle kiss.

The true love of which Jesus speaks is a love of self-sacrifice for the sake of another. This true love is just beginning to emerge for Belle and

Beast. Their courtship is in full bloom, but their experience in self-giving and self-sacrifice for one another has only just begun.

AN UNEXPECTED TWIST

After days of conversations, loving interactions, and an especially romantic night of dancing and dreaming together, Belle and Beast retreat to the ballroom balcony beneath an exquisite, starlit sky. Just when we expect to hear a declaration of love and perhaps even a marriage proposal, Beast inquires after Belle's happiness in the castle. Perhaps "doing for Belle what Beast would have Belle do for him,"[55] Beast wants to know more about her yearnings. He asks from a position of mutuality and equality, without assuming that his royal gifts are any more important than her peasant heart.

During their courtship, he has given Belle many fairytale endings: beautiful gowns, scrumptious meals, romantic music, and servants to attend to her every need. For Belle, an inquisitive lover of books, the best gift Beast has to offer is his magical library—a library containing thousands if not hundreds of thousands of books. Given this fairytale life, Beast perhaps hopes to hear that Belle is happy in her life at the castle. Even viewers who have seen these films many times yearn to forget what they know in order to hear Belle express joy in her new life and affection for this attentive creature at her side.

But this is no ordinary, romantic fairytale. This is a story of lives being transformed through the power of self-giving, even sacrificial, love. For this type of story, a typical fairy tale ending is not sufficient. And so our story continues, bringing more and more people along in the journey toward transformation, and challenging both Belle and Beast to even greater heights of love and self-sacrifice.

In Disney's romantic fairy tales, the princesses' parents and family are absent, forgotten, or seemingly tangential. Not so in *Beauty and the Beast*. In our story, Belle's loving heart fully embraces the father who raised her. It is her father that comes to mind when Beast asks Belle if she is happy there with him. Wondering where he is and what he is doing, Belle laments in the 1991 film: "If only I could see him one last time."[56] With joy that he can meet her request, Beast offers Belle his magic mirror, allowing her to see her father.

For Belle, even a magical life in the castle would be tinged with sadness without the one who raised and cared for her. When she looks in the mirror and sees that he is alone and in danger, Belle yearns to rescue and care for her aging father, regardless of the luxuries she leaves behind to do so. Compared to the greater sacrifices she has already made, this one may be easily overlooked. But in a world that values material belongings and financial wealth over family and life-giving relationships, this sacrifice is worthy of notice. After all, Jesus speaks more about money and the distribution of wealth than he does about prayer and worship—calling us to prioritize love above all else, even the things of this world. There, on the ballroom's balcony, Belle prizes love of family above the wonders and gifts of this magical castle. Surprisingly, we see that Beast does as well in the loving decision he makes.

Much to the dismay of the castle staff who are eagerly looking forward to returning to their human form, Beast releases Belle to return to her father. Now that Beast has finally grown to love Belle fully and unselfishly, he puts her heart's desires and needs above his own. Beast sets her free, as all true love does. God's love invites, but never coerces. In love's invitation, we find ever greater and deeper union with the Source of all love and light. In giving up any hope for his future life as a prince, Beast displays the sacrificial love that Jesus speaks of in the Gospel of John. There is "no greater love" that Beast could have shared with Belle than releasing her to return to the father she loves.

BECOMING WHO WE TRULY ARE

The first time I saw the film, I wanted Belle to declare her joy in castle living, and her love for Beast. I wanted her to take Beast with her as she searched for her father. I wanted Belle to find her father and bring him back to the castle, so they could all share in this magical new life. I had not yet grasped that this was not just a fairy tale, this was a gospel tale—a story of good news, a story of lives transformed by love, a story where shortcuts make for long detours.

Stories have purpose, and this story's purpose is woven around the transformative power of sacrificial love. But if this purpose is to emerge and play itself out in the characters of our story, everyone, including Belle and Beast, has more growing to do. In the midst of this plot crisis, we are reminded that opportunities for heroism do not go away—there will be plenty more right behind them. Moreover, if a hero stops acting heroically, he is no longer a hero. If a hero rests on her laurels when others are in need of her assistance, she is no long a hero. Offering occasional acts of self-giving love can only take us so far. Growth in sacrificial love expands when we take more than just a few moments now and then to give selflessly for others. As our self-giving actions flow from the center of our being, we grow into the beautiful beings we truly are, the beautiful beings we are created to be, and the beautiful beings we are meant to become.

There is an already/not yet dimension to becoming who we are. If this sounds paradoxical, rest assured, it is. It is the realization that mystery lays at the heart of all transformation. The true self is always present, even when operating out of the smaller, ego self. In Judeo-Christian terms, we all bear the image of God within us—an image that cannot be tarnished, corrupted, or destroyed. We are who we are in God's eye, and nothing more—or less! Looked at from one perspective, Beast does not need saving—he already is the beautiful creature God has created. But Beast cannot see it, and certainly does not act in accordance to who he really is; and so, Beast needs to become who he truly is, and who he is meant to become—because by almost any outward measure, he's not there yet.

When asked the simplistic question, "Are you saved?" a theology professor of mine expresses the paradox we see in Beast: "I was saved; I am being saved; I will be saved." Beast was saved by the love that knit his true self together in his mother's womb, and by the image of God that resides within him. Beast is being saved from his smaller self by the transforming effects of self-giving and sacrificial love. Beast will be saved as love's transformation becomes complete and he lets go of his small self to reclaim his true self. As Mufasa says to Simba from the clouds in *The Lion King*: "Remember who you are."[57]

With each moment of growth toward fuller, freer loving, we reflect more brilliantly the sacred image of God within us. And as we travel this heroic, miraculous path of love, and as our light shines more brilliantly, others are able to glimpse, however faintly, the same light within themselves. In such seeing, many are drawn to travel this road with us. And so it is with Belle and Beast as their story continues, even as they travel different roads.

INNER TRANSFORMATION CARRIES A PAIN ALL ITS OWN

With Beast's blessing, Belle rides away from the castle to save her father. In that moment, we see Beast fading away in grief and despair. By releasing Belle to find her father and return to her old life, Beast has seemingly given away his best chance for life and happiness. But even as Beast gives up his own needs and dreams, his beastly appearance no longer reflects his inner life—for that life has become a thing of beauty. Beast has opened a door for larger, more expansive dreams to emerge, but he cannot see it. In opening himself to love, he has opened himself to a suffering unlike any he has known before—for he has lost the one he loves. The pain of his inner transformation, without the accompanying joy of returning to human form, makes death seem preferable to going on as if nothing has changed. For everything has changed. And yet, he will remain a beast in the eyes of the world.

There is a strange truth about self-sacrifice: When we give of ourselves freely and abundantly from hearts of deep love and attitudes of pure grace, our hearts expand, strengthening us and transforming us into brighter, more beautiful beings. But there is another equally strange truth about self-sacrifice: Others will likely see this transformation in us before we do. Beast cannot fully see his beautiful transformation as he laments Belle's absence, knowing he will always be haunted by a love that almost broke the spell.

WE DON'T NEED AN ENCHANTRESS TO BE CURSED

Although this is a fairytale story of enchantments and spells yet to be broken, Beast's predicament points to the truth of a larger story: We become imprisoned when self-centeredness is the force that rules our lives, and when selfish motivations define our decisions and actions. In a world that rewards self-promotion, personal success, and personal gain at the expense of others, self-centeredness and selfishness can easily become the highest values that guide us. No enchantress is required to curse us into following selfish pursuits, neglecting our body's health, denying our soul's higher desires, and turning away from our community's needs. We see this curse in our addictions to food, alcohol, drugs, shopping, and gambling. We feel this curse in isolationist attitudes that have us washing our hands of responsibility for violence and poverty in our world. This beastly curse destroys the very foundation of our lives, as personal gratification slowly erodes our spiritual strength and our capacity for love, grace, and compassion. Without a spiritual foundation of love, grace, and compassion, beauty and light dim and fade.

Beast knows this only too well. Before Belle brought love and beauty into his life, he had no magical antidote to the curse of selfishness. But as his love grows and his self-giving expands, he inwardly becomes the handsome prince he yearns to reclaim—a prince his servants have been pulling for all along.

SERVING OUT OF DUTY

The castle servants have served the young prince his entire life, suffering alongside him during the long years of the enchantress' spell. Faithfully performing their duties, they have cared for Beast, Belle, and one another. While duty and obligation initially drive their service, they eventually find the hope and courage to believe they can save their castle and master.

The servants of Beast's castle are similar to the servants of Jesus' parables, whose lives and roles were defined by the Roman world in which he lived. Servants and slaves serve because they are required to do so. In a hierarchical society, they survive in the lowest levels of power and authority. In Jesus' parables, when these servants perform their duties well, they are merely doing what is required of them. But when they fail to perform their duties well, he uses them as literary examples of moral failure. No wonder preachers and teachers struggle to interpret these ancient parables in ways that are useful and edifying in the 21st century!

Things had not changed significantly when this fairy tale was penned in 18th century France. As in Jesus' parables, these castle characters exist to serve their master. The chain of command is clearly delineated: As master of the castle, Beast has all of the power and authority, whether he deserves it or not. Their loyalty derives from their station in life, rather than any self-giving ethic on their part. The castle servants of this story, however, are remarkable in their sincere compassion and love for their master—even in the face of his cruelty and his responsibility for their enchanted condition.

This had once been a castle filled with servants of all ages and backgrounds, in the tradition of the European Middle Ages. Not quite as dignified as the cast in Downton Abbey, Beast's servants follow a similar chain of command and represent as diverse a make-up as we would find in any 19th century English or French novel. Transformed by the enchantress' spell into common household items, the servants continue to serve their beastly master—loving and caring for him as best they can, despite his beastly temper and their altered forms. Even in their strange circumstances, they function as they had before in their interactions with one another. The head housekeeper, Mrs. Potts, and the chief steward, Cogsworth, debate over "best practices" when Maurice arrives uninvited to the castle. The same disagreements emerge when Belle leaves her room in search of a meal after Beast has forbidden it. The maître d',

Lumiere acts as master of ceremonies and vocal artist for Belle's luxurious feast when he is not flirting with the maid.

Even back in the village, Gaston has a faithful, if sycophantic, sidekick, LeFou, who gives selfless service to his powerful master. For most of the film, LeFou is a jester-like character, always humorous and helpful, serving dutifully as he knows he must. When Gaston pounds LeFou on the head or drops a chair on him, it seems to be more for the benefit of comic relief than anything else. But when LeFou obeys Gaston's command to stand faithfully in snow while awaiting Belle's or Maurice's return, or when he travels into the dangerous forest with Gaston, even LeFou seems willing to sacrifice himself in service to Gaston.

Since ancient times, servants have been used in literature to provide more than entertainment; they convey valuable lessons to those both inside and outside the story. The servants in Disney's *Beauty and the Beast* are no exception. Shakespeare used servants and messengers to forward the plot in his plays, in much the same way Chip forwards the plot in the 1991 film when he asks Belle why she left the castle. For the viewer, LeFou's playfulness takes the sting out of Gaston's cruelty, helping us to laugh and even enjoy his twisted and sinister plots—thus keeping the movie safe for children and fun for adults. Similarly, the castle servants keep us aware of the spell's terrible toll on everyone in the castle—helping us love Beast when he is cruel and angry, making us laugh as Belle and Beast get in a snowball fight, and leading us to cheer Beast on as he learns to love.

EXPANDING IN SERVICE OF LOVE

Their roles and purpose change, however, when Beast's servants assume the duty of defending the castle from the invading villagers. In the siege against the castle, these servants become yet another example of sacrificial love. During the village attack upon the castle, the castle servants display the transformative power of self-giving love, just as Beast and Belle before them. These servants defend the castle with their clever abilities as living household objects, protecting one another time and again. Mrs. Potts and her troop of teacups defend beer steins with their hot tea. Cogsworth saves Lumiere from being melted by sailing down the banister and plunging household scissors' into the rear end of an unsuspecting LeFou, breaking his own strict adherence to proper castle behavior. Lumiere quickly recovers to use his powerful flames to save the lovely maid, turned feather duster, in a quick scene that is perhaps the most typical Prince Charming moment of the entire film. And finally, the knife drawer and stove defend the royal dog, turned footstool, with a burst of flame and operatic cry of power that sends the villagers fleeing in fear for their lives. The castle is saved, but more importantly, the servants show yet another example of sacrificial giving in this story of sacrificial love.

These servants are no longer simply serving out of duty and obligation. After all, when informed of the impending attack, Beast replies dolefully: "It doesn't matter now. Just let them come."[58] As the servants disobey a direct command from their master, they are transformed from servants who merely do their jobs into self-defined warriors—a team of friends and colleagues who work together to save their home and their lives because they choose to do so, without reference to their master.

No Longer Servants, but Friends

These are no longer just servants, these are friends to their master—for they have defended a friend, too weak and sorrowful to defend himself.[59] They have defended his home, risking both their lives, and even their livelihood should Beast decide to dismiss them for their insubordination and disobedience. These servants are more than they were, and can help us delve more deeply into Jesus' parables and proverbs about servants, slaves, and service to others.

These servants have much to teach us—particularly those of us who live with more privilege and power than a 1st century slave or a 19th century servant. Although we may not be trapped in roles that require us to serve others out of obligation and duty, we may be trapped in rigid understandings of what serving God and neighbor actually means. Too many preachers and theologians teach that servanthood is a Christian obligation to be obeyed, rather than a natural outgrowth of love to be cherished. Too many religious leaders depict God as a cruel taskmaster who will punish us when we don't serve frequently enough, perfectly enough, or lovingly enough. Some depictions of God seem more beastly than even the Beast of our fairy tale.

In contrast, mystics and spiritual teachers of every tradition speak of union with God as an encounter with unconditional love and acceptance. As the great mystic, Julian of Norwich, writes: "The Lord looks at us with mercy, not with judgment. In our eyes, we do not stand. In

God's eyes, we do not fall. Both visions are true, but God's is the deeper insight."[60] We can spend our lives in fear of God's wrath, or we can rejoice in God's extravagant welcome and unfailing love. The choice is ours.

When Jesus calls us to serve, he does so in hopes that we will serve, not as slaves to an angry God, but rather as faithful companions of the one who longs to gather us in, as a hen gathers her chicks under her wings.[61] We are called to give selflessly, not out of fear, but out of joyous gratitude. Self-giving love, freely given, does not cause us to lose ourselves, but rather to discover ourselves more fully as we grow into the fuller, freer, more beautiful versions of ourselves. Created as a human being, Beast can only become fully human when he learns to love and give of himself joyfully. Created in the divine image, we become the fullness of that divine image when we love and give in this way, growing in our relationship with both God and neighbor.

We are called into union with God, as friends and companions with Christ. We are invited to serve out of love and joy, not out of obligation and duty. We are encouraged to serve out of faith and hope, not out of fear and trembling. Only then can we grow into self-giving servants who care for the least and the last, who courageously defend the weak and the vulnerable, and who gladly rejoice when others benefit from our gifts of service and care.

PERFECT LOVE DRIVES OUT FEAR

In some parables, Jesus criticizes servants who shrink from their duties out of fear, or who serve out of obligation alone. He expects a frightened slave entrusted with one talent (the equivalent of a year's wages) to make the value of that talent grow. Fearful that he might lose his master's money, the slave plays it safe, burying the talent entrusted to him in the ground.[62] How my colleagues chafe at the ending to this parable, when Jesus says the slave will be cast into the outer darkness! Surely the gentle, loving Jesus we have come to know in Sunday School would never be so cruel, especially to someone who was afraid. Surely a beautiful enchantress would never turn a young prince into a beast for being selfish and unkind. But what if our parable and fairy tale have lessons to teach? What if both stories warn us that we create our own beastliness, and we cast ourselves into outer darkness, when we act out of selfishness and fear. Scripture assures us that "perfect love drives out fear,"[63] but what if the reverse is true as well? What if fear and despair

91

have the power to thwart love's bloom and to paralyze us into self-absorption?

Think of Beast. His inner transformation has awakened his full humanity, and his outer transformation into a handsome prince is within his reach. Yet he hides in the West Wing, paralyzed by grief and despair, while his castle is under attack. The love within him has the power to drive out this grief and despair, but only if Beast embraces this last and greatest power of love. As bereavement counselors often teach: Grief is a process, but recovery is a choice. Love, like God, invites, but never compels. Beast has allowed love to fill his heart. The fullness of its holy and sacred power is in his grasp—but it will not give him courage and hope against his will. Perfect love may drive out fear, but only when we let it. The choice is ours.

FINDING OUR COURAGE—FINDING OUR PURPOSE

Only when Beast sees Belle again and he allows love to burst forth from within, does Beast find the courage and the hope to become fully human again; only then does he grow into the princely purpose he is called to fulfill. In the same way, it is only as the castle servants find their courage while working together and defending their home that they grow into their family-like purpose. Through a common struggle, and the courage required to meet it, the servants rediscover their gifts and purpose as the castle community.

With a renewed sense of purpose, the servants embrace their responsibility to selflessly protect one another and their precious home. Cogsworth, so frightened about rule breaking early in the film, is fearless as he sails down the banister to save Lumiere. Gone is the scared little steward, fearful of disappointing the master, and so worried about Beast's explosive temper. This tiny mantle clock has transformed into a giant grandfather clock of a man—ready to take on the world. Perhaps even ready to take on his master, should Beast remain as lost and fearful as he's been in the past.

Like the servants of Beast's castle, we can find the courage to grow and expand through self-giving love. As we realize that the world we serve is not only God's world, but also our world, we recognize that this world needs our gifts and our giving. What a joy it is to love and serve, when we realize that the people we are called to love and serve are not just God's people, they are our people!

We are, after all, one human community, living on one planet earth. Together we share a common purpose: to strengthen our community through love and service, and to take care of our planet. Sharing a birthright as God's children, we are not just *servants* to one another, we are *family and friends*. We are not just servants to our God, we are partners and reflections of God's very image. We are blessed by the divine Spirit in our lives, that we might be a blessing to others. When we bless God, we bless one another. When we bless one another, we bless God. When we bless God, we bless God's world. When we bless God's world, we bless God. Funny how that works.

We are intimately connected in ways that are impossible to fathom. Just as Beast's servants are drawn into his fateful enchantment, they are blessed by his transformation into the beautiful being he was created to be. And just as we are drawn into one another's sorrows, and failings, we are also blessed by every act of transformation that brings beauty and sacred power into our lives and our world.

WHEN FEAR LEADS US ASTRAY

When Belle leaves Beast to save her endangered father, all three are drawn into a tragic situation. While Beast sinks into despair and laments the loss of his beloved, Belle is so fearful of losing her father that she cannot perceive the danger her village poses to herself, her father, and to Beast. Belle's family crisis turns tragic, as Gaston whips the community into a frenzied mob, and has Belle and Maurice imprisoned so they cannot warn Beast of the villager's impending attack. In trying to save her father, Belle has simply exchanged one form of imprisonment for another. Worse yet, after rescuing her father from incarceration in Beast's castle, Belle now finds herself the cause of her father's imprisonment at the hands of a man who looks like Prince Charming but who acts like a beast.

It is worth pondering that this story might have unfolded very differently. If Beast had not found it in his heart to release Belle and had kept her as his prisoner, Gaston might have been the true hero of this story: risking his life to rescue the poor maiden locked away in an enchanted castle. But Beast does find it in his heart to release Belle, and Gaston does not have the heart of a hero. As Belle pleads for her father's freedom, the plot twists unexpectedly. In trying to protect her father from Gaston's evil plot, Belle inadvertently endangers Beast, by showing Gaston and the villagers Beast in the magic mirror.

93

As Gaston hears Belle's loving depiction of Beast and sees the affection in her eyes, Gaston plays on the villagers' fears, riling up the crowd to fear and hate this beast who might one day terrorize their village. Playing upon their passions, Gaston inflames the community's suspicions and stereotypes about magic, beasts, and the danger of the unknown. We are often quick to fear those we do not understand; and we are far too ready to sacrifice those we perceive to be a threat. Fear can lead us astray, blinding us to the chance of transforming an adversary into a friend or ally—a friend who might bring joy to our lives and to our world. Without the courage to expand and grow, our journey toward transformation may be delayed or even blocked, and the world may miss out on a beautiful blessing.

No one in the early church believed that Saul, who persecuted the early Christian community, was anything more than an evil man to be feared and loathed. No one would have believed he could be transformed through an encounter with love and grace on the road to Damascus into the greatest evangelist the church has ever seen. A dead Saul could not have become the Apostle Paul, who wrote so much of the New Testament. A dead Beast could not have transformed a cursed castle or become a blessing to the territory in his royal care.

THE FINAL SACRIFICE

When Belle races back to the castle to warn her beloved Beast and his castle servants, she cries out to Gaston for mercy as he stands poised to take Beast's life. At the sound of Belle's voice, Beast awakens from his grief-filled despair, and with something now to live for, defeats Gaston and suspends him by the throat over the castle wall. Looking into Gaston's eyes and perhaps recognizing the lost soul he has recently been, Beast realizes that he is no longer a beast and refuses to act like one. Seeing this enemy through the eyes of his transformed heart, Beast's anger is transformed by empathy and understanding. In this transformation, we begin to glimpse the heroic prince within—a prince that has been emerging since love's transformative power took seed and began to grow.

As Beast offers compassion and mercy to Gaston, a new type of self-giving love transforms the cruel beast into a kind-hearted warrior. The artistry of the animation and acting is powerful in this scene— Gaston devolves into a frightened little boy with huge eyes, desperately seeking mercy, while Beast's face grows gentler and smoother. Beast's eyes, formerly crinkled in anger, now open in wonder and reflection, as they see Gaston with new-found empathy—perhaps even recognizing similarities between their two lives.

As Gaston begs for his life saying, "Please, I'll do anything!" Beast places him back on the tower balcony with the simple command: "Get out." Beast's kindness is not a foolish one. He does not invite Gaston to dine with them or even remain in their presence. He merely spares Gaston's life and returns him to stable ground, offering him safe passage away from the castle.[64]

But no good deed goes unpunished, and as Beast and Belle reunite with joined hands, Gaston proves he is the true monster by fatally attacking Beast from behind—falling to his death in the process, the victim of his own bloodlust. As with Jesus and so many others who have shown compassion and mercy to their enemies, Beast is betrayed by the one who received mercy and loving grace. Belle tries to save Beast for the second time, pulling him to the safety of the tower, but Beast's wounds are beyond her power to heal. As Beast lies dying, Belle sobs over her lost love. Beast has sacrificed his happiness by letting his beloved Belle go, knowing it will likely mean being trapped in his beastly form forever. This sacrifice has brought Gaston to the castle to kill him. When Beast sacrifices his revenge by sparing Gaston's life, Gaston repays mercy with malice. Now, as Beast lies dying atop the castle tower, Belle holds on with gentle caresses and words of hope and healing. Still, her words are not enough, and she is forced to watch Beast die before her very eyes.

TRANSFORMATION: A RESURRECTION STORY

Even in the face of death, Belle's love is not defeated and works a powerful magic all its own. Unlike other Disney fairy tales where romantic love saves the day, true love's kiss is not the source of Beast's salvation. The love that saves Beast comes from a much deeper well. Belle's love not only encompasses the best of Beast, it includes every facet of his being, even that heartless adolescent boy who once rejected an old woman in need. It is said that God loves us, not because God's perspective is limited to our best qualities, but because God's sees the totality of who we are. We can only hate or despise others if we only see a slice of their lives. Belle's love is strong enough to break the spell, bring Beast back to life, and transform her friend into a handsome young man precisely because Belle has learned to see with the eyes of her heart enlightened. Belle's tears of compassion and words of love are sufficient to save the day and bring the one she loves back to life. Before our very eyes, Beast is transfigured and resurrected from a dead beast into a living, breathing man.

In this magical scene, I am reminded of Jesus' beloved friend Lazarus who lay dead in a tomb for many days before Jesus arrives. This is the occasion for scripture's shortest passage: "Jesus wept."[65] Did Jesus weep out of compassion for Lazarus' sisters, out of grief for his friend's death, or out of sorrow for his disciples' lack of understanding? We know not why; we only know that he weeps over his departed friend. Weeping, praying, and calling Lazarus forth, Jesus brings a dead man out of a tomb where he had been lying for several days. This is no mummy that emerges, but a living, breathing man, covered in burial clothes— clothes that Lazarus' servants must remove if he is to walk among the living.

What are we to make of this tale of Lazarus' resurrection? I am reminded of Ezekiel's vision of a field covered in dry bones. When asked by God if these bones can live, Ezekiel responds: "God, you alone know."[66] The truth is, we don't know. What we know is that from a depth of love for a friend, Jesus calls forth life. What we believe and what we are willing to hope for make all the difference in the world. This is the power of the gospels and fairy tales like *Beauty and the Beast*. These stories convey a truth about the power of love and compassion— a power that can bring forth new life where death seems to hold sway.

The miracle of Beast's resurrection story is further enhanced by the enchantress' reappearance in the 2017 film. Even though Belle proclaims the holy words, "I love you," after the rose's last petal has fallen, the enchantress offers a beautiful moment of gracious compassion as she infuses the dead rose with the mystical power of life, blessing the prince with the transformation of form he so richly deserves. Belle personifies this same care and compassion in her teary declaration of love—a declaration that elicits an explosion of magical light, transforming the prince from a lifeless beast into a living man.

True to the fairytale genre, our story has a happy ending—with servants celebrating their return to human form, Belle and Beast dancing their way into marital bliss, and Belle's father joining the castle family. The gospels follow a more complex path, as Jesus' sacrifice leads to a long, arduous death and many days in the tomb before any sign of life emerges. But in the miracle of Easter, transformation and joy reign, as

Jesus' resurrection brings new life and new hope to everyone touched by his life.

Learning to give of ourselves is a lesson that unites the gospels and our fairy tale. Beast's transformation occurs because of this precious lesson, and in Beast's life-giving transformation, others are saved, transformed, and blessed. This is the gift of sacrificial love and self-giving attitudes: We save others. We transform others. We bless others. And in the process, we are saved, transformed, and blessed.

THE TRANSFORMATIVE POWER
OF COMMUNITY

Not Just One Hero

There is not just one hero in any life story. We are all blessed and gifted by a myriad of people who guide us, teach us, mentor us, inspire us, and even save and help transform us. Fairy tales are different, however. Most fairy tales have one knight in shining armor or one moment of miraculous transformation—a moment when good overcomes evil, a hero saves the day, and a happy ending is achieved. In the fairytale genre, *Beauty and the Beast* is rather unique in its journey toward transformation. For it is a tale with many heroes and saving moments—moments that impact entire communities as the story concludes. This is a complex tale. The enchantress' spell is a broad-reaching one, and it will take more than one hero to effect the necessary transformations required to break it. After all, it takes a village to raise a child—or save a beast.

The two communities in *Beauty and the Beast* are central to its story line. Both the provincial village and the castle community harbor agents of change, but they also hold characters in need of transformation. In the most powerful tales, communities are either formed or transformed by their heroes and villains. Disney's classic fairy tales, however, seldom portray this communal transformation. More frequently, they focus solely on the hero and heroine, or prince and princess, who must find one another, escape evil, and seal their love with a happily-ever-after ending. Disney's *Beauty and the Beast*, meanwhile, provides a very different story line, weaving in poignant stories and songs from supporting characters and communities. These characters and communities are not window dressing; they are central to the story, adding richness and depth to the tale. Achieving a happily-ever-after ending requires more than the happiness and fulfillment of one young couple, it requires the happiness and fulfillment of an entire kingdom.

COMMUNITIES IN NEED OF TRANSFORMATION

From the film's prologue, we discover that the entire castle community is "groaning in travail,"[67] awaiting restoration. For Beast is not the only one under enchantment; his stewards, housekeepers, maids, cooks and even the castle dog share the prince's fate, and are fully invested in Beast's transformation. Only when Beast learns to love and to receive love in return can the lives of Beast and the servants be transformed and their humanity be restored.

Belle's little French village, in contrast, seems perfectly normal and predictable. A first glance might suggest that this quaint little town is simply a launching place for our story—the typical Disney backdrop with a gorgeous landscape and non-descript characters with no significant role in the story. But transformation and change eventually define both the castle and the village, bringing these communities front and center with important roles to play.

There is an unusual kinship between Belle's village and Beast's castle community—neither is what is appears, and yet both are somehow related. Initially, Belle's kind and simple village seems blessed—an almost idyllic small town in its clear self-identity and predictability. In the 2017 film, Belle's father admits that their little village is a bit "small-minded," but "small also means safe," he explains.[68] Even knowing that this small village might not be a perfect fit for his family's creative outlook, Maurice chooses this village as the perfect place of safety and security for raising his daughter.

Beast's castle community, by contrast, seems cursed rather than blessed. Trapped in a dark, dreary castle, forced to live as household objects rather than as human beings, this community is in obvious need of transformation. Seldom is a community's need for its leader to grow to his or her heroic potential so clearly and poignantly portrayed. We can't help but chuckle at the end of the 1991 film when Chip, who is no longer a teacup, asks his mother, Mrs. Potts: "Do I still have to sleep in the cupboard?"[69] But his question reminds us how deeply tragic this story could have become had Beast not grown into his best possible self through the transformative power of love. As the 2017 film comes to a close, this potential tragedy is visibly portrayed as the servants-turned-household-items say their final good-byes to one another and fall into an enchanted sleep like Sleeping Beauty's kingdom—forever to remain in their cursed forms. The enchantress' spell acts like a Greek tragedy, claiming the humanity of everyone in the castle, even wiping the memories of loved ones in the village beyond. The spell impacts the entire kingdom, not just Beast and Belle.

Bringing Community to the Forefront

Sleeping Beauty is the only other Disney fairy tale that portrays a community under enchantment. But neither Disney nor Grimm helps us fall in love with *Sleeping Beauty*'s community. For the community is peripheral and plays no real part in the story. This community is quickly put out of mind as we watch the dramatic story of a beautiful princess, a wicked witch, and a handsome prince. Even when the entire kingdom is put to sleep, to awaken only when princess Aurora awakens, this community is barely seen. It certainly isn't transformed by the experience: Aurora's father, the king, is foolishly confused; her mother, the queen, simply smiles silently; and the kingdom's residents fade into the background as Aurora and Phillip—her prince who has come and awakened her with true love's kiss—dance off into the clouds of "happily ever after." Even as the romantic ending for princess Aurora and prince Phillip is exalted and emphasized, the community's century-long sleep is portrayed as nothing more than a trifle. This is hardly surprising, for in a world of fairytales, community plays virtually no role in the stories.

Disney fairy tales usually focus on two individual characters who have a few sidekicks and supportive best friends of their own. Cinderella and Prince Charming are surrounded by members of his kingdom who stand mute and unmoving as the couple dance and fall in love. Even Cinderella's stepmother and stepsisters fade to the background as she waltzes away to her happily ever after. In *The Little Mermaid,* Ariel and Eric save one another and seemingly unite two kingdoms, as they fall in love and marry. But those kingdoms are peripheral as the story of their courtship unfolds. Even in animal tales like *Bambi* and *The Fox and the Hound,* other forest animals are relegated to the roles of sidekick and background scenery.

In sharp contrast to this fairytale pattern, the community of characters in *Beauty and the Beast* plays a predominant role in the Disney films. These characters remain popular and beloved 25 years after the animated film's release. Walk past the Lego Store's *Beauty and the Beast* display in Downtown Disney and you'll see Lumiere and Cogsworth standing alongside Belle and Beast. Review any list of Disney gifts and artwork for *Beauty and the Beast* and you'll see portraits of Cogsworth and

Lumiere along with tea sets of Mrs. Potts, Chip and the other teacups. We have grown to love these characters every bit as much as we love Belle and Beast. We grin at their clever attempts to bridle Beast's temper, and we cheer as they help Beast receive Belle's friendship in hopes she can break the spell. Even as we laugh at their antics, we yearn for their transformation back into human form. The castle community stands front and center throughout the film. In the 1991 classic, Belle could not have returned to the castle in time to save Beast if teacup-Chip had not stowed away in Belle's bag and used Maurice's invention to break down the cellar door. There is nothing peripheral about these castle servants.

As we watch Belle and Beast become friends, we smile with the servants in the warm glow of love's slow bloom while they sing: "There may be something there that wasn't there before."[70] We grieve with them as Belle rides away, and cheer with them as they battle the villagers to protect their castle. We want this community to experience transformation every bit as much as we want Beast to do so.

THE LINK BETWEEN PERSONAL AND COMMUNAL TRANSFORMATION

The need for transformation in Belle's little village isn't as obvious initially. Simple though they may be, the villagers seem safe enough. But when the villagers succumb to fear and bloodlust, disregarding any affection for Belle and Maurice, the village's need for transformation becomes abundantly clear. Under the sway of Gaston's rhetoric, these seemingly kindhearted villagers rise to violence, intent on killing the beast and destroying his castle—despite Belle's assurances that Beast is kind and gentle. The villagers of this "safe, idyllic community" are eventually transformed into a hateful mob—a mob far more terrifying than a beast roaring in a mirror could ever be. We know this story well, for we have all seen people morph into the worst versions of themselves when threatened or challenged.

This film rejects the simplistic portrayal of communities in earlier films like *Sleeping Beauty*. Neither the castle servants nor the village neighbors are static, muted, or even predictable as our story develops. Each community offers positive and negative examples and lessons; each community exhibits its own wisdom and folly. As the villagers become intent on killing Beast and his servants-turned castle objects, we are reminded how easily hate and fear can maim the spirit of a community—turning even the simplest and kindest of us into something ugly and monstrous.

Compare the villagers' descent into mob hysteria with the behavior of the castle servants. By all rights, these castle servants could have grown angry and resentful toward Beast over the years. After all, his selfish attitudes and behaviors had gotten them into this mess. Yet, their hearts remain pure, their love remains loyal, and they continue to serve faithfully and selflessly. In the 2017 film, Mrs. Potts explains that they stay with Beast to make amends for the years when they did nothing to prevent him from growing into the beastly young man he had become before the spell.

Her explanation points to a key element in both Beast's story and in real-life stories of transformation. Our communities can play a big role in personal transformation, both positively and negatively. A community can assist our ascent to higher levels of awareness and greater acts of love and compassion or can help facilitate our personal demise. The castle community chooses the role of helpful assistant as they nurture and strengthen the love growing between Belle and Beast. Eventually, they even protect Beast's hearth and home from another community's attack. The castle residents turn out to be heroes in our story, while the residents of Belle's quiet village turn out to be rogues and knaves.

Community is an equally important aspect of the gospel story. One of the most powerful impacts of Jesus' ministry is the formation of a world-changing community. What began as a small group of Jews following Jesus grew into a politically and religiously significant community of Jews and non-Jews working together to live and teach the lessons of Jesus. As a world religion, Christianity has built and toppled kingdoms and influenced and transformed leaders around the globe. At their best, Christian communities have strengthened and changed the world for the better. At their worst, Christian communities have deepened divisions among peoples and nations. Jesus and his message, and the communities that follow both messenger and message, have become intrinsically linked. It's hard to fathom successfully separating the two.

Similarly, in our tale, the fate of Beast and his servants is intrinsically linked from the moment the enchantress places a spell upon the castle. This linkage points to the powerful truth that human transformation never occurs in a vacuum. When we change, grow, develop, and even transform, we do so in relation to other people in our lives. As the young prince becomes more and more beastly, his community does nothing to prevent his demise into cruelty and selfishness. But as this community embraces their role and responsibility as mentors and guides, Beast begins to grow more human again. As Belle befriends her captor, and as Beast develops kindness and compassion, the castle community embraces hope again—working ever more faithfully toward the transformation needed by one and all.

Analogously, communities are impacted by even slight changes in the lives of its members. The greater these changes are, the greater these changes have on the community. Our own ability to transform is highly impacted by the relationships surrounding us, just as our personal transformation impacts the transformation journeys of the communities and individuals in relationship with us. Supportive friends may plead with us to "never change;" insisting that they love us "just the way we are." (Think back to your high school yearbook messages.) At the same time, supportive communities can provide a foundation of strength from which we can develop and grow. The perseverance and loyalty of Beast's servants support him through years of darkness and despair—laying the foundation that loving transformation was still possible. Their loyal support keeps Beast's hope alive, ready to embrace its chance when a loving young woman stumbles upon the castle. Beast's community builds upon this supportive foundation after Belle arrives by inspiring and encouraging Beast to foresee a better future, to perceive his best possible self, and to live into his potential with hope and courage.

THE GIFT OF COMMUNITY: SEEING POTENTIAL

This is the gift of community—seeing the possibility for something better in one another, and encouraging the transformation necessary to bring it about. Bringing out the best in one another is a gift we can offer every relationship we are in. The creation story of Genesis 2 proclaims, "It is not good for the man to be alone."[71] Humans are created to be in relationship, to live in community. Our ability to work together, grow together, and adapt with the seasons of our lives has allowed us to survive in the past and strengthens us to thrive in an ever-changing world.

As Beast's community works together, they are able to help him see himself differently, and to imagine new possibilities. They strengthen his faith and hope, encouraging him to develop behaviors that will draw out the man trapped inside a beast's body. As Belle perceives Beast with the eyes of her heart enlightened, she too becomes part of his community of encouragement. In turn, Beast does the same for Belle. Together, they strengthen one another on this transformative journey of new understanding and mutual affection—even as they are supported by a castle full of servants who surround them with strength and encouragement along the way.

Two Are Better than One

Early in Jesus' ministry, he surrounds himself with twelve named disciples and dozens of other followers who travel with them. Forged into a close-knit community, the disciples travel in pairs to do the work Jesus was doing in the world. To their great surprise, they are able to teach and serve and heal in miraculous ways—in ways they wouldn't have believed possible. Depending on the account, Jesus sends either twelve or seventy-two to serve in this way. Most scholars surmise that many others remained behind, supporting the ministry pairs with funds, food, and shelter upon their return. Jesus forewarns them not to waste their time with those who do not receive them and their service; these disciples are told to "shake the dust from their feet" and move on to communities who will.

Jesus' advice is instructive: We shouldn't waste our time trying to help those who don't want to be helped. The disciples clearly take this advice to heart, for when they return from their travels, they are energized and enthusiastic about the deeds of power and acts of love and healing they are able to offer while working together. As Ecclesiastes says: "Two are better than one, for they have good return for their labor."[72] When we seek to achieve transformation by ourselves, the task seems daunting. But when we seek the same transformation in community, the task seems almost easy. When we work together, the return on our labor far exceeds the sum of our individual efforts.

Researchers have discovered that Canadian geese flying together in v-formation are able to travel 70% farther than they are able to fly on their own. The geese honk their encouragement to those in front, as they break the wind and provide lift for the geese flying behind. When the lead goose tires, it drops back to the rear of the formation where the resistance is lightest, while another goose moves up into lead position. And if a goose is injured or becomes sick during the migration, two other geese will stay behind to protect it from predators until the goose either recovers or dies. This is the power of living and working in community.

104

By working in community, we develop a synergy that unlocks new worlds and the creative awareness of how to access those worlds. The divine image within each of us connects together to shine more brightly when we help one another broaden our perspective, raise our awareness, awaken new perceptions, and strengthen the courage of our love. Perhaps this is exactly what Jesus means when he says, "Where two or three gather in my name, there am I with them."[73] For the light that shines within us when two or three gather together far exceeds the light we can shine on our own. You and I may be the light of the world, but our individual light is tiny in comparison to the light *we* create when we shine as the light of the world together. Just as an enlightened community shines a mighty light to brighten the world, a supportive community illuminates the transformative road of love.

WHEN COMMUNITIES RECEIVE OUR GIFTS, EVERYONE GROWS

Communities receive and reject opportunities for growth and transformation, just as individuals do. While the religious authorities try to turn the people against Jesus, his life and teachings continue to bless the communities around him. Lepers and prostitutes receive his healing and guidance. Mary Magdalene is not only healed by Jesus of multiple demons, she joins his close group of followers, becoming one of the only female disciples named in scripture. Tax collectors, like Matthew and Zacchaeus, transform their former lives of usury and self-absorption into lives of compassion and generosity. A motley group of fishermen become healers, teachers, miracle workers, and spiritual leaders in their own right. The more they embrace the transformative love and teaching of Jesus, the easier their continued growth in faith and love becomes. As they grow together in their understanding of and relationship with Jesus, their ability to help others grow and transform expands.

This is the truth of transformation. Every act of personal and communal transformation lays the foundation for further growth. Personal transformation strengthens the potential for communal transformation, and communal transformation supports the journey toward personal transformation. When we help others, we are strengthened ourselves. When communities support our individual journeys toward transformation, we move forward more quickly and grow more steadily. We expand to new and unimagined heights through the power of community.

CREATING LIFE-GIVING TRANSFORMATION

Growth leads to more growth, just as contraction leads to more contraction. Change occurs in either case, but when we embrace life-giving transformation, we create the conditions for further life-giving transformation—both individually and communally. We see this in Beast's castle community. When we first meet these strange creatures, we encounter a community that has adapted to their unusual circumstances. Lumiere continues to romance the woman he loves, even if she has become a feather duster. Cogsworth still runs the household with dignity and dependable efficiency, so worthy of his clockwork form. These servants remain unfailingly loyal to their master, even if he has been outwardly transformed into a beast. Their adaptability creates its own sort of community transformation, as they forge a new castle community.

Even as they sleep in cupboards or hang out on tabletops, these servants embrace the fullness of their humanity, continuing to serve their master as they had before the enchantress' spell. Rather than despairing and fostering anger or resentment, they dream of a better future when they will be "human again." As they longingly dream of a better future, they hope to help transform their prince's beastly heart into one capable of giving and receiving love. Just as the servants dream of becoming human again, they dream of helping the prince become fully human for perhaps the first time in his life, as he grows into a compassionate man with a loving heart. This community yearns for Beast's transformation as deeply as he does, and its support is an example to all who seek to support one another on our journeys toward transformation.

The servants' love and compassion for Beast has remained steadfast over the years. Indeed, it may have even expanded—for while they are still gentle with him, they are also firm in ways that were probably missing during his youth. When Belle arrives at the castle, they openly and honestly express their hope that she may be "the one" to help Beast break the curse. They are equally open and honest about their expectations that Beast not give up on himself or them. The servants' hope grows, and their optimism for the future expands, as they help Beast court young Belle—encouraging the friendship growing between them.

As the castle community embraces hope, they strengthen Beast's self-confidence. As they radiate hope and enthusiasm for the future,

Beast's wariness fades. And as the servants offer Belle hospitality and encouragement, her comfort and joy also grows. The castle servants even strengthen their resolve to help Beast control his temper. Perhaps strengthened by Belle's courageous personality, Mrs. Potts and Lumiere lecture Beast in the finer points of anger management, reminding him that he must learn these lessons if he is ever to earn this beautiful woman's love. Slowly, Beast receives their lessons and opens himself to their gift of hope. A loving friendship forms between this strong-willed woman and this impatient beast, in part because they accept the support and guidance of the castle community.

To Grow or Not to Grow

Growth begins with a choice. At some point, Belle and Beast must decide if and how their relationship will progress. Will they allow themselves to continue to grow with each new awakening, or will they pull back? Will they allow the changes they have experienced to become the foundation for future growth and transformation, or will they resist the change? These are questions we all must face when confronted with opportunities for growth and transformation. Will we lean forward into the unknown and embrace forward growth, or will we turn back toward the familiar and shrink to our former selves? The choice is ours.

The same questions can be asked of communities. Will they support our journeys toward growth and transformation, or will they pull us back into old, familiar patterns, even if they purport to hate those patterns? Visit any Alcoholics Anonymous meeting and you'll hear as many stories of families supporting addiction as those supporting recovery.

To grow, or not to grow; that is the question. Communities are just as likely to resist growth and change as they are to encourage it— perhaps in the foolish hope that stability can guarantee predictability. Whether the community is a family, a neighborhood, a town, or a group united around a common purpose, communities that resist growth and change are communities that choose death and self-destruction over life and rebirth. Ironically, it is the communities that try to avoid change who suffer the most when change is thrust upon them. Change is unavoidable, but the choices we make can help determine whether this change is life-giving or death-dealing.

WHEN COMMUNITIES HOLD US BACK

Human communities are funny things. Unlike Canadian geese, most people don't like flying in formation. When a goose falls out of formation, it immediately feels the increased wind resistance and the loss of lift from the bird ahead and will quickly move back into formation. This is rarely true of people. Some people pride themselves on their pioneer spirit and on going it alone. Other people have no interest whatsoever in making another's life easier. Sometimes it's even challenging to know which communities and relationships are supportive and life-giving, and which ones are not. Communities that appear kind and loving may in fact be cruel and judgmental. Communities that appear antagonistic and challenging may in fact be supportive of growth and transformation. Not all communities are interested in expanding perspectives, deepening perceptions, growing love, and embracing life-giving transformation.

And, of course, communities (including communities of faith) are not static. Communities that once thrived and served the world with passionate purpose and loving generosity can experience declining membership and turn inward. Becoming obsessed with not losing additional members, faith communities can turn self-protective and self-absorbed; spending more time reliving the "glory days" of the past than offering love and service to anyone outside of their walls. At the same time, families that had once been filled with dysfunction and sorrow can break free of their destructive patterns to emerge beautiful and loving—embracing transformational growth as they learn to appreciate, support, and love one another.

Like Belle's village and Beast's castle, it is not always clear in the gospels which communities are being transformed like butterflies and which ones are being hardened like concrete. Nazareth is Jesus' hometown, the place where he grew up in love and safety. But this all changes when this quiet community becomes offended by his teachings in the local synagogue. Jesus' neighbors find his prophetic preaching so offensive they chase him out of town with the intention of throwing him off a cliff.[74] Belle's relationship with her hometown is equally complicated. At first the villagers praise her beauty and begrudgingly admire her aloof independence, even as they fail to understand her. But when they feel threatened by Beast's appearance in the magic mirror, they lock her away as they seek to destroy the new life she has embraced with her beastly friend.

As their hometown children grow into adults of transformative love and revealing light, both Nazareth and Belle's village resist growth and transformation. Rather than receiving Jesus' and Belle's love and light as gifts, and embracing the promise of growth and change these gifts bring, both hometowns harden their hearts and close themselves off from the power of transformation. In the Gospel of Mark, Jesus says: "A prophet is not without honor except in his own town, among his relatives and in his own home."[75] In Disney's *Beauty and the Beast*, Belle says it this way: "It's just that I'm not sure I fit in here."[76] In Nazareth, Jesus cannot perform the miracles for which he is so famous. In Belle's little village, she is both admired and ridiculed for her love of books and her daydreaming ways. Even when she tries to teach a young girl to read in the 2017 film, the schoolmaster chides her. He can't imagine why would girls need to read, let alone invent washing machines or think for themselves!

In a world filled with rising crime, civil unrest, and an outbreak of bubonic plague, Maurice chooses this small village to raise his young daughter because it seems safe. While provincial and small-minded might be a strange fit for his creative temperament, Maurice chooses the safety of this town over one that would be more open to creativity. Perhaps Joseph and Mary made a similar decision in settling in their hometown of Nazareth after returning from Egypt. Nazareth was a small town, far away from the centers of Roman power and Jewish politics—a town where they could raise their mysterious child in relative anonymity.

Parents around the world raise their children in similar communities, hoping to provide their children this same sort of safety and security. Over time, however, if our hometowns resist our efforts to grow into the fullest versions of ourselves, they can transform from warm, swaddling clothes in a cradle of love to cold bonds of confinement. The tight wrap of that warm cradle is no longer comforting. As our dreams urge us to look through the bars and to strain against the familiar limits, we begin to push back against efforts to keep us small—until we finally crawl up and over the barriers into a broader world filled with expansive possibilities.

GROWING BEYOND THE BORDER

Even in Jesus' early years, he crawls up and over the barriers of convention—wandering away from his family caravan during their annual pilgrimage to Jerusalem, and remaining behind to listen and learn in the temple. Jesus even pushes against the barriers of temple life at the tender age of twelve, as he questions the priests and proclaims his own knowledge and wisdom. The heroes we admire often push these limits early in life, as they yearn for a larger worldview than the one they were born into.

As we yearn to know more, as we strive to grow, and as we seek to answer God's call in our lives, our expanded worldview leads to more yearning, striving and seeking. As we stretch the boundaries that seek to hem us in, small towns and hometowns can entangle and trip us up. Even people and places that nurtured us in the past may limit us moving forward—urging us to limit our dreams and shrink back into old patterns of behavior. Perhaps we understand this more clearly as teenagers than at any other time in our lives. Even Jesus rebels in his 12th year. Without notifying his parents, Jesus remains behind in Jerusalem to question and debate with the temple elders. Later in his ministry, Jesus advises his followers to become as children if they hope to enter God's kingdom. Jesus seems to understand that there is more to childhood than childlike innocence. Growing up requires us to move beyond existing barriers. Teenagers realize instinctively that they must push against the limits of old patterns, and create new paradigms if they are to define themselves in adulthood. To fully grow, we all eventually push against and move beyond familiar barriers—learning to grow in new ways and make our own discoveries. This adventurous quality in children and teenagers is easily lost in adulthood, but is essential if we are to successfully embark on journeys of transformative growth.

As Belle yearns for more than her childhood village can offer, she sings her truth into the void: "There must be more than this provincial life."[77] New people, new places, new experiences, new adventures call her away from her small town. Inquiring of her father, "Do you think I'm odd?"[78] Belle confesses she doesn't really fit in. Somehow, her hometown isn't feeling like home. She yearns for something more. Yet, when Maurice finally gets his invention to work, Belle doesn't join him as he sets off for the fair. Instead, she remains behind in her little house inside the borders of her little village. As much as we want to break free, it's hard to actually leave. Even the adventurous Belle doesn't ask to accompany her father on his journey into the wider world.

Jesus' childhood experience couldn't have been that different from Belle's. Surely Jesus outgrew Nazareth long before he left town around the age of thirty to begin his ministry.[79] What was it like for this amazing man of God, this messiah, miracle worker, healer, wise guru and teacher, to be confined in Nazareth for so long before embarking on his ministry? What was it like for his community to know they raised a man beyond their ability to understand?

DIFFERENT FROM THE REST

A man of such mysterious beginnings and mystical power would be unusual in almost any town of any size in any century—but Jesus must have been particularly enigmatic in his tiny, first-century Palestinian town. *The Infancy Gospel of Thomas*[80] imagines stories of this unusual child—a child who brings dead creatures and even a dead friend back to life, but who also curses another child and blinds his parents. Can't you just hear the whispers that must follow him, as they follow Belle through the town? Like Belle, Jesus must have been a puzzle and a mystery to the people of his small village. We can even imagine them singing of this strange but special young man the way Belle's village sings of her.

Like Jesus, Belle would be an unusual young person in just about any town of any size in any century—but particularly as a young woman in a small rural town living in a century not known for supporting free-thinking, imaginative dreamers. Preferring books to vapid conversation, Belle eludes the understanding of Gaston and most of the town. Girls Belle's age think she's crazy for rebuffing Gaston's wedding solicitations. I suspect they're equally puzzled by her lack of interest in clothing, makeup, and local gossip. The daughter of an inventor, Belle herself is a visionary, transforming the stories she reads into dreams and visions for her own life. She looks out at the mountains and sees great adventures, imaginative possibilities, and limitless opportunities. This visionary outlook is not celebrated in her little village.

Imagine the village receiving Belle as a gift and guide! Might they have grown with Belle, appreciating her wisdom as she learns and develops her creativity? Might they themselves have experienced transformation as they blessed her and supported her dreams, gifts, and inventions? Instead, they resist and reject everything that makes her who she is—everything that might have blessed them with opportunities for growth and transformation.

Rejecting Old Roles to Make Room for the New

The villagers use "strange," "peculiar," and "different from the rest of us," to describe Belle's refusal to play the roles they expect her to play. The only child of an eccentric inventor, with no mother to lean on, Belle is expected to accept the duties of housekeeper, caretaking daughter, and eventually nursemaid to her aging father. Seen in this light, it's not far-fetched that Gaston foresees himself as her Prince Charming. In a typical country village, his wealth and strength would be highly valued by young women seeking protection from poverty and social disgrace—particularly for a motherless young woman with an eccentric, risk-taking father. Fortunately, Belle's father appreciates her creative spirit and does not try to marry her off to secure her future. In the live action re-make, Maurice tells Belle that she reminds him of her mother—another woman equally fearless and ahead of her time.

In first-century Nazareth, Jesus surely faced the same sort of role expectations. A first-born son like Jesus was expected to follow in his father's footsteps, care for his mother and younger siblings, and take over the family business when his father was too old to do so. Like Belle's proficiency as an inventor and artisan, Jesus' knowledge of scripture and his theological acumen indicate proficiencies far beyond the roles his community expects him to play. Jesus has clearly dedicated a significant amount of time to rabbinic study and religious pursuit. The rabbinic life would not be a normal path for such a child—particularly one whose mysterious beginnings carry some questions of legitimacy. Certainly, becoming a traveling rabbi is not on his hometown's agenda for him. Imagine Nazareth receiving Jesus as their local rabbi! Might they have grown with Jesus, appreciating his wisdom as he learns and develops his ministry? Might they have benefitted by blessing him and supporting him as he moves on to share his gifts with the world? Instead, they resist and reject.

Life-giving teachings can open up new possibilities and lay the groundwork for growth-filled transformation. Amazing leaders can inspire us to expand and grow as we aspire to deeper love, greater fulfillment, and more active participation in making the world a better place. The opposite, however, is equally common. Even the most life-giving teachings are often rejected in favor of old, familiar patterns. Even the most wonderful people are often hated for the bright lights they shine—a hatred that can stoke anger and fear, and can lead to an ugly transformation.

Ah, but when we receive this light and allow it to connect with our own inner light! We can then create a brightness that reveals new truths, new opportunities, and new hope! When communities gather together as their best possible selves shining their light, they create a brilliance that outshines clouds of despair. They light a path toward beautiful transformation for all who bask in their light. When we choose to grow, we can admire the new blossoms that emerge and celebrate the new worlds we create.

Like Jesus before her, Belle yearns for a path of life-giving creativity and transformative growth. In order to embark on this journey of growth and expansion, she must eventually leave this small hometown community that is incapable or unwilling to celebrate her unique gifts. And so Belle must find a new community—a community that will support and nourish her growth; a community that will receive the gifts and creative spirit she has to offer.

FINDING NEW COMMUNITIES ALONG THE WAY

Belle's journey away from home initiates her process of life-giving transformation, and she discovers a community to support her on her way. As with Beast's transformation, her journey begins in crisis. She embarks on her adventure into "the great wide somewhere"[81] in order to save her missing father. When Belle leaves her town and home behind, she is not rejecting her community or going on a personal journey or Vision Quest to find herself. Nor does she run away from home to seek the adventures for which she yearns. She leaves to search for her father, who is lost and in danger. Like Jesus before her, Belle wanders out into the world with a self-giving purpose. Her courage becomes a gift that will help her find her father and, unexpectedly, a new community of support. But in this quest to seek and save another, she finds and saves herself in ways she might never have imagined or experienced otherwise.

Many of us are best able to answer our calling and embark on the path toward life-giving transformation when we step out of our comfort zones and away from our familiar hometown communities. By leaving their hometowns behind, Belle and Jesus find the freedom to live into their higher calling, discover and develop new communities of support, and grow into their authentic selves. When Jesus leaves his familiar hometown to wander looking for the lost sheep of Israel, Jesus discovers the wide world's many aspects—not all synagogue-safe experiences, but also wilderness temptations and dangerous encounters with other religious leaders. He heals the sick, welcomes the outcast, and embraces the leper, and forms new communities of faithful support along the way. By leaving her warm home to look for her lost father, Belle also discovers a much wider world—a world of not only heart-pounding adventure, but also dark caverns and dangerous paths. She discovers that she can talk to clocks and candelabras; she can forgive a monster and embrace rather than fear an enchanted castle. With expanded perceptions and perspectives, Belle discovers that a loving being can hide behind a monstrous façade, and that a man may actually be hiding inside a beast.

Only in leaving that little house in that little town can Belle discover the higher truth she needs in order to grow and mature into the beautiful, powerful woman she is capable of becoming. And only in leaving that family home in that family town can Jesus discover the higher truths he needs in order to grow and mature into the miraculous messiah-savior he is capable of becoming.

For many of us, we answer our calling best and embark on the clearest path toward life-giving transformation when we step out of our comfort zones and away from our familiar hometown communities. Even within the familiar walls of his home castle, Beast leaves the seemingly safe and familiar world of anger, fear, and despair to enter Belle's world of creative dreaming and hope-filled living. Entering that new world, even within the confines of his castle walls, allows him to journey forward to the life-giving transformation he has so desperately yearned for while living under a spell.

In stepping across that threshold from familiar to unfamiliar, growth-filled discoveries present new learnings, unpredicted revelations, and miraculous abilities that strengthen us to become the amazing people we are capable of becoming. Our perspective changes with each new vista we encounter; our perception expands with each new experience. As we move toward transformation, we find new communities of support, and expect even more from the communities who first nurtured us, as we journey to new adventures.

FINDING A COMMUNITY THAT EMBRACES TRANSFORMATION

Discovering communities that will support us is a challenging journey in and of itself. Discerning which communities will embrace and encourage life-giving transformation and which will resist and discourage growth is more challenging still. A closer look at the two communities in *Beauty and the Beast* reveals clues and wisdom to guide our way. It's important to ask: What brings these communities joy? What do they celebrate? Where do they place their focus? Contrast the boisterous bar song of Gaston's village, celebrating Gaston's narcissism and small-mindedness, with the castle's joyous song of hospitality, inviting Belle to be their guest.

After Gaston comes up with a plot to have Maurice thrown in the local asylum if Belle continues to rebuff his advances, LeFou and chorus sing to thunderous applause:

No one plots like Gaston
Takes cheap shots like Gaston
Plans to persecute harmless crackpots like Gaston....
My what a guy, Gaston![82]

When a community finds joy in the ideas of persecution and cruelty, it's a pretty safe bet this community does not, and will not, embrace growth and transformation.

Compare the villager's gleeful anticipation of Gaston's cruelty, to the castle servants' joy as they offer Belle hospitality and help alleviate her fear:

You're alone
And you're scared
But the banquet's all prepared
No one's gloomy or complaining
While the flatware's entertaining . . . .
Be our guest![83]

When a community finds joy in offering hospitality and comfort, it's a pretty safe bet this community embraces growth and transformation.

WE GROW WHAT WE FEED

These brilliant lyrics of Howard Ashman reveal a truth about the journey of life: We grow what we feed; and we move toward the source of our joy. Where we place our attention and focus, and what we choose to feed, will determine where we end up in life. The same holds true for communities. Communities that focus on hope and love create a world of hope and love. Communities that focus on narcissism and self-interest create a world of narcissism and self-interest. Which of the two wolves will we feed? The appetite of narcissism and self-interest? The hunger for power, prestige, and popularity? Or, the yearning for hope and love? The thirst for friendship, hospitality, and compassion? The appetite we feed determines the feast we create—a feast of love and transformation, or a feast of anger and resentment.

When Gaston feeds the angry and fearful wolves within his fellow villagers, they rise up in hatred to attack and destroy everyone in the castle. The fact that the cruel beast within their souls can be roused so quickly indicates how frequently these villagers have been feeding this beast. Eyes that once twinkled with mirth now narrow in bloodlust. Voices that once sang sweetly and gently of a mysterious girl now chant a vicious battle song. In the 2017 film, LeFou sings of the monstrous turn of events as he marches alongside Gaston. Seeing the dangerously ugly transformation in Gaston and his fellow villagers, LeFou quietly wonders who the real beast truly is.

In sharp contrast to this village community, the castle servants have been caring for one another during the hard years of their enchantment, feeding the gentle wolves inside themselves. Having grown in their own beauty of love and light, they are more bonded than ever as they gather together to defend their castle and their master. With the angry and fearful wolf within kept unfed and in check, these servants have no desire to harm the invading army—they simply want to drive them off so that they can live to see another day, and move another step toward their dream of becoming human again.

Likewise, Jesus is no stranger to ugly transformations. The joyous crowds that sing "Hosanna to the son of David" as Jesus enters Jerusalem transform into an angry mob a few days later shouting: "Crucify him!" We see these crowds throughout human history: crusaders marching in anger against cities and leaders of foreign religions; medieval villagers hunting down alleged witches and burning them at the stake; Hitler youth bullying their Jewish neighbors and destroying their shop fronts, cheering as they are rounded up and sent to the gas chambers; Ku Klux Klan lynch mobs inciting violence and burning churches.

The angry mob in *Beauty and the Beast* is a reminder that angry mobs are a very real part of our world. If we want to grow, both individually and communally, we must remain diligent. We must feed the gentle wolf within ourselves, attend to our higher selves, and listen to the love and beauty within—lest we become the beast that resides right alongside the beauty in each and every one of us.

Don't Be Deceived by Appearances

Whereas the villagers in Belle's hometown shrink from love and become an angry mob intent on death and destruction, the castle community grows and expands in both love and loyalty, as conflict and fear intensify. How we respond when threatened defines not only who we are, it shapes who we become. Those who respond in love, faith, and hope are transformed in life-giving ways, while those who respond in hate, fear, and violence are transformed in ways that lead to self-destruction and death.

While the village community has the appearance of a good and safe place to raise a family, it reveals itself to be a community capable of great cruelty. And while the castle community has the appearance of a cursed place ruled by a horrible beast, it reveals itself to be a community blessed with love, light, and generosity of spirit. The enchantress' words ring as true at the end of the film as they do at the beginning: "Don't be deceived by appearances, for beauty lies within."

The Beauty of Transformational Communities

This reality is seen in communities around the world, some beautifully transformed and others not. Transformational communities reflect the beautiful love that great religious leaders like Jesus taught and lived. This beauty grows exponentially when embraced by a community. As the community grows forward toward more life-giving transformation, lessons received are expanded and leaders broaden their impact as more of love's beauty is created and shared.

The beauty of the gospel does not end with Jesus' death. Rather, it expands to reach even more people. With Jesus' first resurrection appearance to a small group of women, hope is reborn in the midst of death. Soon, many disciples are embracing and proclaiming the good news of life-giving transformation. Jesus' earthly ending was only a beginning to the fullness of the gospel story. Howard Thurman writes that the work of Christmas begins after the Christmas celebration ends. For, the work of Christmas is the work of Christ: the work of loving God and neighbor. Jesus embodied this message and inspired others to travel the same loving path, living this message each and every day:

To find the lost,
To heal the broken,
To feed the hungry,

To release the prisoner,
To rebuild the nations,
To bring peace among people,
To make music in the heart.[84]

The true beauty of any journey of transformation is most clearly revealed in community. Belle grows more beautiful with each passing scene, as she embraces love and compassion in new ways, and Beast discovers both his ability to love and the beauty that resides within his very being. This is the way of love: Love begets love. Our dreams continue beyond us, and our growth continues in the lives we influence and impact.

The work of Dr. Martin Luther King, Jr. did not end with the signing of the Civil Rights Act of 1964, nor did his dream die with his death in 1968, for his dream was not just the dream of one man, it was the dream of a community striving for a better world. Long after Dr. King's death, his work continues moving forward. Dr. King's dream envisions a beauty far beyond the banning of public segregation, for his vision looks toward a world where justice rolls down like waters and where the rights of all extend without regard to race, color, religion, sex or national origin. More legislation has been passed and additional advocacy work has ensued, even as calls for justice and equality continue. This dream continues today, embodied by religious communities, legal organizations, social agencies, justice advocates, community organizers, political lobbyists, public servants, and individuals who work diligently to forward the cause of justice and inclusion.

What if Dr. King had only preached to a small congregation in the countryside of Georgia? What if his influence had only reached the population of his home church in Atlanta? The world would not be the one we know today, for Dr. King's life and teachings are inextricably linked with that of his followers, even with that of his enemies. The world is a better place today, not just because of Dr. King's life and teachings, but because of the communities who embrace his teachings, embrace his legacy, and nourish non-violent journeys of communal transformation. Communities who have followed Dr. King on his personal journey of transformation and those who continue to forward his dream today are creating communal journeys of transformation that have and will forever change our world into a more beautiful place of loving inclusion and justice-seeking for all.

The work and teachings of great leaders like Dr. King, Mahatma Gandhi, Mother Theresa, Muhammad, the Buddha, and Jesus are impactful beyond any one person's force of personality or personal journey toward transformation. Their work and teachings are powerful because of the way they are embraced by communities on journeys of transformation. Their work and teachings create transformational journeys for others, and continue to guide and nourish transformational journeys around the globe—journeys toward greater beauty, fuller life, and expanded love for all the world. These leaders, just like Jesus before them, proclaim the beauty that comes from within—the beauty that arises from love and justice. This beauty shines forth as we live into our highest purpose and become our fullest selves of love and light.

This is what it looks like when communities embrace transformation. At their best, transformational communities of all types embody this Great Commandment to love God, and to love our neighbor as ourselves. As Hillel notes: "Everything else is commentary."[85] When communities focus on compassionate love and transformative growth, they show their truest beauty for all to see.

A COMMUNITY LOVE STORY

The communities of *Beauty and the Beast* need to discover the truth of inner beauty every bit as much as do Belle and Beast. For, this is not just the love story of a girl and a boy; this is a love story of a whole community. They are on love's journey toward transformation together. Beast and Belle are growing, supported by the castle community; the castle community is changing, inspired by Beast and Belle. Beast's transformation is intimately intertwined with the transformation of his community. The fate of Beast and his servants are inextricably linked each and every step of the way.

Long before Beast is fully transformed, the castle community is already being transformed for the better as they bathe in the light of Belle and Beast's growing love. Beast's transformative journey of learning to love transforms his community so fully that they are firm in their loyalty and strong in their own confidence when the villagers come to attack. Without question, the castle residents gather together to defend hearth and home, even when their own master is fading back away into despair and hopelessness. The castle community's faith has grown, and they are unshakeable in their intention to save both Beast and their castle. As they prepare to defend their beloved home and their beloved master, the light within the castle servants shimmers brightly, highlighting the unexpected beauty of their calm confidence and fierce loyalty.

Even as they win the castle battle, the castle servants know the only real victory lies in supporting Beast's transformation. Both Beast and his community know they are dependent on one another, connected together on this journey toward wholeness. Nowhere is this seen more poignantly than when Lumiere, Cogsworth, and Mrs. Potts look on in disbelief and indescribable grief as Beast lies dying on the tower floor. Having successfully driven off the invading villagers and seeing Belle return to the castle, their salvation is surely at hand. But now, the master who has finally learned to love and who has regained his humanity is dying. All hope seems lost. In the 2017 film, the servants seek to comfort one another as the last petal falls, sealing their doom forever.

They do not see Belle plead for Beast not to leave her, or hear her speak the words "I love you," just before the last petal falls. If the love within Belle's heart lifted the spell, transforming the servants back to their human selves, but did not bring Beast back from the dead, would the servants celebrate their freedom, or would they view it as a pyrrhic victory? Free from the spell with access to the castle's vast wealth and the prince's sizeable fortune, released from the obligation of taking orders from the prince who was responsible for their plight to begin with, can we imagine these servants living happily ever after? It seems inconceivable, because it's not who they are; it's not who they have become through the long process of growing together as a community and through helping the prince truly become human again.

Beauty and the Beast is a community love story because no one in the castle can be happy unless all are happy. No one can be fully transformed unless all are transformed. On that tower, Belle proclaims her love for Beast and unleashes the powerful magic that will not only save and transform Beast back into the prince he has become, it will transform everyone in the castle back to their beautiful human forms as well. The castle itself is transformed from a dark and sinister place crumbling in ruin into a place of beauty and light.

Like Jesus on the mountaintop with Moses and Elijah[86], there on that tower landing, Beast has a transfiguration experience. Beast is visibly different, surrounded by light and beauty. Like Jesus, Beast's transfiguration is seen only by his closest friend, but it is a transfiguration that affects his entire community. Maurice, Mrs. Potts, Chip, Lumiere, Cogsworth, Belle, Beast, and even the prince's faithful dog

120

gather together as one community to celebrate the tale of true love that has grown and transformed them all.

The story of *Beauty and the Beast* is a tale as old as time, not because it's the story of two people falling in love, but because this is a story of transformation. This is a story of the life-giving transformation that changes people, communities, and even the world. For even as Belle and Beast dance toward their personal happy ending, we know this happily ever after includes everyone in their new community—a community celebrating, loving, and interacting, just as they have been doing for the last two hours as we have watched this love blossom and grow before our very eyes. Community lies at the very heart of our story, just as it lies at the very heart of every transformation in our lives and in our world.

THE JOURNEY TOWARD
TRANSFORMATION

Just a little change
Small to say the least.[87]

Every day, we experience a little change here and there: We find ourselves an inch taller or a quarter inch shorter depending on our season of life; we notice our a baby's first golden locket or a friend's first gray hair; we get hired for our first job or enter into retirement; we stand transfixed before a rising sun or a setting moon; we see life stir within a blooming flower or fade within a falling leaf. We experience changes both big and small every day. Some of these changes are permanent; others are as fleeting as a shooting star. But even small changes can initiate larger opportunities for growth, and even permanent changes don't automatically bring true transformation. When we embrace growth, new blossoms emerge, creating beauty in the gardens of our lives. By inviting life-giving change and growth into our lives, we embark on the beautiful journey of positive transformation—a journey with as much power to enrich our lives as it did for a village girl named Belle and a prince known as Beast.

But how do we invite this life-giving change into our lives? As we see throughout the story of *Beauty and the Beast*, it can't simply be the nature of the change—for while changes in one person's life lead to transformation, the same changes in another's life do not. Are there clues that explain how and why some people experience amazing transformation, while others do not? To answer these questions, it will be instructive to explore both the conditions that make journeys toward transformation possible and the tools that aid our individual and communal journeys.

THE GROUND OF TRANSFORMATION

Life has Lessons to Teach

Life has lessons to teach us. Love and suffering seem to be the two great paths toward transformation—suffering grabs our attention, and love lights the way home. While we would prefer the path of love, some lessons arrive most clearly along the path of suffering. If we flee from the pain of these lessons or if we hunker down and ride out the storm without being transformed through the process, the lessons inevitably come around again—usually more insistent and harder to ignore.

Moments of brokenness can create fertile soil for the seeds of transformation to begin growing in our lives. Life's misfortunes can be good teachers if we are willing to pay attention. We may be stuck in a joyless life, working a j-o-b that fuels neither our souls nor the dreams we have long-since buried. We may be in a loveless relationship, too accustomed to going through the motions to know that we can reach for more. We may not like where we are stuck, but when misfortune strikes (an accident, an illness, the death of a loved one, or loss of a job) and our situation becomes intolerable, we often open ourselves to real transformation. Trials offer opportunities for learning, for reclaiming hope, for exploring new possibilities, for re-inventing ourselves, and even for creating life out of the ashes of defeat and death.

The prologue of *Beauty and the Beast* takes place in a castle filled with servants and the sort of privilege that offers our young prince everything he needs to grow into his princely role—everything *except* the conditions that make transformation possible. Perhaps the young prince is spoiled and over-indulged by doting nannies and loving parents. Perhaps both parents and nannies neglect to teach the young prince the obligations of princely leadership and virtue. The 2017 film depicts the prince suffering at the hands of a cruel father after the untimely death of his mother. This suffering might have led to the transformation of his heart, but instead, it simply hardened it. It's important to note that while love and suffering are necessary conditions for transformation to occur, they are not sufficient in themselves to bring such transformation to fruition.

Whatever the back-story of *Beauty and the Beast* may be, personal misfortune is the impetus for our prince's journey toward life-giving transformation. Only after the enchantress turns him into a hideous beast is he willing to receive critiques of his behavior and begin making the changes necessary for genuine transformation to occur. His vacuous noble friendships, his decadent self-centered life, and his cruel attitude toward the world have entrapped him in a beastly life, and it is only when his outer form is transformed to reflect the beastly life within that he experiences enough pain to face his need for transformation. Understanding Beast's journey, in the midst of our own misfortunes, can help us embrace similar journeys of our own.

Love and Misfortune Contain Seeds of Transformation

That Beast's journey toward transformation begins with misfortune is beyond doubt. Getting transformed into a hideous beast is not on anyone's bucket list. But what is not as obvious is that the enchantress plants seeds of Beast's transformation within her spell. She plants the seed that love must grow in order for transformation to occur. For it is only through the prince's learning to love and earning another's love that the spell can be broken. Just as a seed lies sleeping in earthen darkness awaiting the sun's light to awaken it, so too the enchantress' seeds lie sleeping in Beast, awaiting Belle's light to bring them to flower. Misfortune, depicted in our story as the beautiful enchantress, may plant the seeds of transformation within us, but nurturing their growth is up to us.

Whatever seeds of transformation have been planted, very little growth or life-giving change seems evident when we first meet Beast in our story. For almost a decade, Beast has lived with the spell, seemingly with little or no change in his life or behavior. His temper, despairing attitude, and lack of kindness toward strangers remain unchanged. Beast is cruel to Maurice and later to Belle when they arrive unexpectedly at the castle. Even Beast's loving servants seem incapable of shining enough light to awaken the seed buried deep within. But they are capable of helping Belle shine her own light and of making sure she helps thaw the frozen earth in Beast's heart where seeds of transformation have already been planted.

As with misfortune, love may plant the seeds of transformation within us, but nurturing their growth is up to us. If misfortune is like a tsunami warning, love is like the soft glow of Lumiere's candelabra drawing Belle up the castle steps. Ready to the light the way, love calls always. We can choose whether to follow the glow of this light or to remain in the shadows. Though he has known love, Beast has chosen the shadows of self-absorption over the light of love. In the 2017 film, Mrs. Potts tells Belle about a loving mother who drew the young prince to her bedside as she lay dying, only to have the prince's father take him from her side. Her love has nurtured the soil in the boy's heart, planting seeds of hope, promise, and transformation deep within. But the king's cruelty leads the boy to wall off his heart to protect himself from further pain. After his mother's death, the young prince seals his heart from the powerful light of love—the very light that could have reached the seeds of transformation planted by his mother. Yet, once planted in our souls, love can never truly die. Even hidden in the shadows, love waits expectantly for us to break down our walls of fear and doubt and receive the healing kiss of its warmth and light. The seeds of transformation that love has planted in our hearts may lie dormant for decades, but they patiently await the moment when another's loving light will awaken them from slumber.

Planted by the One who is the Source of Love and Love itself, these seeds of transformation are always with us, always available, always prepared to gift us with the power and grace to grow. The gift of love, so essential on the journey toward transformation, has been with Beast from his very first breath. And so it is with each of us, created by Love from the beginning of time. The seeds of transformation are present, ready to grow, even as Beast dwells on the fading petals of a dying rose. But there are secrets to the universe that Beast does not know, including the secret gift of growth—for we are created not for death, but for growth; and we do not travel the journey toward life-giving transformation alone or unaided.

The Universe Pulls Us Forward

The universe pulls us forward, yearning for our transformation. Religious traditions speak of this reality in different ways. Hindus, Buddhists, and Jainists speak of this force as *Dharma*; Taoists call it the *Tao*; and Christians speak it as the work of the Holy Spirit. Perhaps the most compelling description comes from Judaism. The Talmud speaks of a heavenly medium (or *mazal*) that imparts spiritual influence to all earthly things: "Every single blade of grass has a corresponding *mazal* in the sky which hits it and tells it to grow."[88] The enchantress' spell hits the prince with blunt-force trauma. Perhaps she is the *mazal* telling Beast to grow in love, while promising transformation in the wake of love's bloom. The Talmud's forceful language portrays the dramatic nature of transformation more honestly than its paraphrase in popular culture: "Every blade of grass has an angel that bends over it and whispers,

'Grow.'" The enchantress' spell is no gentle whisper; this misfortune is a dramatic call to action. Perhaps Belle is yet another *mazal* bringing the power of transformative love—this time with that gentle whisper of kindness accompanied by the bold strength of stubbornness and wit. Love and misfortune are both powerful, but the *mazal* in love is gentle, while the *mazal* in misfortune can be brutal. Growth is a beautiful thing, but it can also be a full contact sport.

Just as we must choose between embracing the possibilities of life's trials and tribulations, or stirring the dregs of our suffering, so too we must choose between accepting a *mazal's* gifts, or closing ourselves off from its promised growth. Even after the traumatic events that transform the prince into a monster, Beast resists the *mazal's* invitation to love. Buried deep within the soil of Beast's anger and resentment, the seeds lie dormant until Belle and her father enter Beast's life. Perhaps the seeds of friendship Belle plants are so quick to grow because they meet the seeds of transformation already lying within, simply awaiting Belle's light of love to stir them from sleep. Perhaps the castle community has prepared the soil of Beast's life with their self-giving love, moving the old seeds around a bit, and perhaps even planting a few seeds of their own.

TOOLS OF TRANSFORMATION

A journey of a thousand miles begins with a single step.[89] These words of Lao Tzu are as true for the journey toward transformation as they are for any other journey in life. Transformation is a process, and may prove to be long and drawn out, but it begins with a single step. The path is not always clear, and the forward motion is seldom straightforward or simple. When we seek life-giving transformation, we are invited onto a journey with many twists and turns. We may embark on this journey from many different starting points, but start we must if we are to embrace change and the opportunities it presents for our lives. For our journeys toward transformation to be successful, a few tools will help us along the way.

Tool 1: Choice

The first tool to aid our journeys toward transformation is *choice*—a tool so obvious it is often overlooked. As every bereavement counselor knows, grief is a process but recovery is a choice. Not everyone

126

experiencing grief chooses to move from anger to acceptance. In a similar way, not everyone who experiences love or suffering and feels the *mazal's* pull will choose to embark on the journey toward transformation. Make no mistake, we are always on a journey of one kind or another; it is the choices we make that determine which type of journey we will travel. Will we move forward or backward? Will we move sideways or remain stuck? Will we climb the next hill or try to find a way around? The way forward leads to life; the way backward leads to death. Always, the universe pulls us toward transformation, urging us to choose life.

When Beast sees this young woman sacrifice herself to save her father, a glimmer of surprise flits across his face. Just a little change begins to form in this brief encounter with a young woman who loves her father selflessly and sacrificially. The light calls to the darkness, stirring the seeds lying within. But the light can only call—we must choose to answer the call and let the light in. When we choose to let the light in, the seeds of transformation open and sprout. And in this magical movement within the heart and soul, other dormant seeds of transformation are stirred from sleep. These seeds seem to bloom out of nowhere, much like the poppies that bloomed unexpectedly over the battlefield graves in Belgium, France, and Gallipoli during World War I.[90] Just a little change has occurred in what will eventually become a seismic transformation for both Beast and the entire castle community.

Any transformation, seismic or otherwise, begins with a choice to let in the light. But this choice is no more predictable than it is likely. We see this throughout the gospels. Jesus plants seeds of hope and shines God's light of love, offering nourishment with each encounter, but some people and communities choose to embrace growth and transformation, while others do not. Most Pharisees reject his teachings and resist his leadership, but a Pharisee named Nicodemus so longs to feel the warmth of Jesus' light that he sneaks out at night to question Jesus over what it means to receive the life-giving transformation he offers. Making a different choice than his colleagues, Nicodemus is so transformed by his journey with Jesus that he follows him until the bitter end, tending Jesus' body and laying him in the tomb.

In another transformative account, a woman with an issue of blood for much of her life chooses to literally reach out to Jesus for help—touching the hem of Jesus' robe as he passes by in a crowd. Feeling power flow from him and perceiving the woman's faith, Jesus stops to bless and fully heal her. The life-giving change she receives is as transformative for her as Beast's resurrection-transformation is for him. By choosing to reach out for healing, this woman is restored to fullness of life in her own transformation story. In a society where menstrual bleeding is deemed unclean and ugly, this woman is once more beautifully free to participate in her community.

Contrast her choice to reach out to Jesus for healing with Judas' choice to take his own life after betraying Jesus to the religious authorities. When Judas regrets his betrayal, rather than reaching back to Jesus—who has received, welcomed, forgiven, and healed so many— Judas chooses to run away and commit suicide. By choosing death, Judas creates his own tragic ending—an ending that might have resulted in life-giving transformation had he simply chosen to embrace the very one who had healed, forgiven, and transformed so many lives before Judas' very eyes.

Tool 2: An Open Mind

The second tool to aid our journeys toward transformation is an *open mind*—a mind ready to embrace new perspectives along the way. As our perspectives expand and open, our paradigms will change. The foundation underlying our growth may even shift. When Beast almost dies saving Belle from the wolves, her perception of him changes. Perhaps he is someone worth getting to know after all. As Beast befriends this beautiful young woman in his castle, his perception of her expands as well, causing a resulting shift in his perspective on peasants from the village. As these changes invite new perceptions and new ways of viewing his future, Beast grows ever more hopeful, playful, and happy. His lament and despair melt away under the warmth of friendship and joy.

Likewise, Maurice's prejudice against Beast is turned upside down when he hears his daughter's tale of Beast's new-found kindness and gentleness. And when the townsfolk imprison Maurice and Belle, he is surprised to find that a dark and enchanted castle may be a far safer place for his daughter than his familiar village. As Maurice's perspective on safety and fear change, he begins to perceive the beauty and possibilities that Beast and his enchanted community present for Belle's life. From the vantage points of new perspectives, each party is able to see beyond appearances to the beauty that lies within. Only with an open mind can our perspectives embrace the truth that there is beauty within each person. Only with the eyes of our heart enlightened can we perceive the divine light within each of us yearning to shine forth—for we are all created in the image of the Divine.

Tool 3: Awareness

The third tool to aid our journeys toward transformation is *awareness*. By raising our awareness, we begin to perceive things we haven't noticed before. When we consciously take note of what we are noticing, our perception grows and expands. Awareness reveals new paths and new insights to help us determine our direction. This expanded perception becomes a compass to help us chart our way. As Belle and Beast walk together, play together, read together, and even dine together, Belle begins to see that Beast is not so beastly after all. There is sweetness and kindness within him that she has not perceived before. Belle is even able to perceive affinities they share, like good literature and dancing. Even when she views Beast howling in the enchanted mirror near the end of the film, Belle is no longer frightened by what she sees. She is able to perceive grief and loss in the sweet face of a friend, rather than fear and anger in the face of a beast.

Beast's awareness has been growing and expanding alongside Belle's. He notices Belle's friendly gestures and recognizes her playful nature, enticing him to engage in snowball fights and literary debates. With new-found hope and receptivity, Beast hears the encouragement and guidance of his servants, receiving their advice and smiling broadly as each step forward brings him one step closer to Belle. In the 2017 film, Beast realizes he has misjudged the enchantress' motive in giving him a magic book that allows him to go anywhere in the world. Since he will be certainly feared and hunted anywhere he might go, Beast thinks the gift is exceedingly cruel; but to Belle, it is a treasure beyond price. For through it, she is able to discover the mystery of her mother's death in far off Paris. With clearer perceptions and heightened awareness, Belle and Beast are free to move toward loving transformation.

Where we place our attention often determines what we see and where we take our next step. If awareness is perception's first role, interpretation is its second role, and flows from it. How we interpret what we perceive greatly influences the direction we travel. If we perceive possibilities, we are likely to take risks, choose unknown paths, and embark on new adventures. But if we perceive only roadblocks, we may stop or even turn back. We may miss alternate paths, or a chance to clear the road. If, as we look deeply into things, we perceive beauty and life and love, we are drawn farther along the path of life-giving transformation. But if we perceive only entanglement and disappointment, we are likely to miss the opportunity to untangle the situation or weave it into a rope to guide us back to the path of growth and expansion. When we clearly perceive the light that is there to guide us, we see the beauty that is within and around us. On the other hand, when we focus on the shadows that obscure our vision and sap our vitality and strength, we often miss the opportunities for resurrection yet to be revealed. When awareness leads us to follow the light, our expanded perception directs our steps forward.

Tool 4: Hope

The fourth tool to aid our journeys toward transformation is *hope*. In the midst of life's trials and tribulations, our ability to muster hope has a huge impact on whether we embrace growth or not. Will we embrace the possibilities these trials and tribulations bring, or will our suffering make us angry and resentful? Either way, we end up feeding one of the two wolves within. Will we feed our fears and anger? Or will we feed our hope, forgiveness and compassion? Which eyes will we look through as we gaze at our lives and our world? Will we look with the eyes of love and hope? Or will we look with the eyes of distrust and doubt? Will we see creative new opportunities inviting us into a limitless future, or will we see only lost chances pulling us into a prison of "what ifs"?

While Beast focuses on lament and desolation, his castle falls into deeper darkness and destruction. As our story begins, Beast is stuck in his dark, crumbling castle. Trapped in the prison of his mind and the closed doors of his heart, Beast has lost all hope for himself and for his castle community. The only motion forward he can see is toward death and despair. But as Belle forces open the doors to Beast's heart, her contagious optimism and creative imagination bring hope to the castle. As Beast cautiously embraces this gift of hope, he moves outside the walled off world of self-absorption to embrace the beauty that awaits. Inspired by Belle's enthusiasm and joyous outlook, Beast is drawn into playful adventures in the snow, long afternoons pouring over books, and experimental evenings at the dinner table. Anger and temper turn to wry wit and humor, as Beast and Belle tease each other and laugh together, discovering joy's power to nourish hope and optimism.

Tool 5: Self-Giving Love

The fifth tool to aid our journeys toward transformation is *self-giving love*. This tool is necessary if we are to reach our highest levels of transformation. As we give of ourselves, a deeper path is cleared and we enter new levels of being and becoming. In our fairy tale, self-giving love both initiates and profoundly strengthens Belle and Beast's journeys toward transformation. Belle begins this journey by leaving home in order to save her father; Beast begins it when he risks his life to save Belle. As they offer and receive help from each other and from other members of the castle, their giving natures expand and their lives are united in the bonds of love. Each new moment of selflessness plants another seed of transformation in their lives.

When Jesus speaks of eternal life and the kingdom of God, he is not just or even primarily talking about heaven. He is speaking about the inner transformation that comes through self-giving love: "Sell your possessions and give to the poor, and you will have treasure in heaven. Then come, follow me."[91] Give to everyone, care for others, lay down your life for your friends, and love your enemies. For in these acts we sow and water seeds of transformation within the gardens of our hearts and souls. Add the fertilizer of gratitude, then sit back and watch the garden explode with new growth.

Tool 6: Gratitude

This brings us to the sixth tool to aid our journeys toward transformation: *gratitude*. As Belle and Beast begin expressing gratitude and offering small kindnesses to one another, their friendship blossoms. Their ability to both give and receive love and friendship begins to bloom. As we reach upward with gratitude and reach outward with self-giving love, the divine spark within ignites our souls and moves us toward life-giving transformation. In this movement of gratitude, we not only bond with those who receive our love, we bond with God and reflect the image of God within.

Moving forward in gratitude makes our journeys toward transformation clearer and easier to navigate. "Every valley shall be raised up, every mountain and hill made low," proclaims the prophet Isaiah. "The rough ground shall become level, the rugged places a plain."[92] Gratitude smooths our path, drawing us ever closer to the life-giving transformation we seek and to the One who creates us for the fullness of life we discover on our journeys toward transformation.

131

Tool 7: Friendship

The seventh tool to aid our journeys toward transformation is *friendship*. As our bonds with both God and community grow, our journeys are supported by the love of friendship—a love with a power all its own.

As we have seen, misfortune alone cannot create life-giving transformation. How we respond to the tragedies and challenges of life determines the path we follow. For misfortune to sow seeds of life-giving transformation, we need the nourishment and strength of friendship. True friends are a blessing, for they shine light on our darkest journeys and unveil hope in our deepest despair. Even this blessing of friendship and community is sometimes not enough. Despite the castle servants' best efforts to reach the seeds of transformation buried in Beast's heart, he shields himself from the light of their love and sinks back into the listless despair and self-absorption that defined his life before the spell. It is not until Belle's arrival that Beast drops his shields, allowing a ray of light and a burst of energy to nourish the seeds of transformation lying within. As friendship grows, so do the seeds of transformation that have been planted in Beast's life. Seeds, soil, people, and relationships—in the midst of misfortune, all four elements are required to call forth a process of life-giving growth and transformation.

This tool of friendship becomes one of the most nourishing aspects of our growth toward transformation. The transformative friendship between Belle and Beast is further strengthened by their castle friendships. The servants-turned-enchanted-objects share wise advice, offer loving support, and provide them with an ever-hopeful perspective. Maurice, Cogsworth, Lumiere, Mrs. Potts, and even Chip are important friends and guides along Beast's and Belle's long, winding journey toward transformation.

Though these servants yearn for their own transformation every bit as much as they long for their master's, their offers of friendship are not selfishly motivated; they flow from the core of their being. Faux friendships have no more power to aid our journeys toward transformation than does a kiss from a prince who only seeks a princess' hand to gain a kingdom. All love is holy, and God will not be mocked. While the love of friendship may not be as powerful as unconditional love, it is certainly as powerful as romantic or erotic love. As friendship blooms between Belle and Beast, new life emerges, hope springs forth, and love begins to blossom. Only through the powerful love of friendship can transformation reach everyone in the castle.

This community of loving friendship works alongside our own powers of perspective and perception, calling us to give lovingly, generously, and even sacrificially. For friends help till the soil in the gardens of our hearts, calling forth life from the seeds that are blooming on our journeys toward transformation.

Tool 8: A Spirit-Guide

The last tool to aid our journeys toward transformation is a *spirit-guide* to help us on our way. Throughout history, spirit-guides have had many names and taken many forms: Christians call on Jesus, saints, and angels; Jews look to *Sophia* or the *Ruach Yahweh*; Muslims submit to the will of Allah; tribal and native peoples call on their ancestors, animal guides and spirit-helpers for help; while fairy tales look to fairy god-mothers, wizards, or enchantresses to lead the way.

Spirit-guides should not be confused with the universe's pull toward transformation. The latter is an impersonal force like gravity, while the former is intensely personal and interested in our individual journeys toward transformation. In the 2017 version of Beauty and the Beast, the enchantress Agathe is this spirit-guide. After casting the spell on the castle, Agathe remains nearby in the woods as a peripheral member of the village community. Agathe is always watching, perhaps even protecting, but seldom intervening. But when she intervenes, it's magical—much like people's experiences of God![93] It seems Agathe is the one who sends Maurice to the castle, as he wanders lost and frightened in the woods. Perhaps she knows that Beast's time is coming to a close, and another dramatic intervention is necessary if his journey toward transformation is to move forward. When all hope seems lost as the last petal falls *before* Belle confesses her love to her beloved Beast, Agathe returns to the castle. Compassion and power emanating from within, Agathe sweeps the lifeless petals back into a rose shimmering with new life. This life heeds the love Belle confesses to Beast, calling him back from death and transforming him into the prince he has long since become on the inside.

Keep Moving Forward

The universe pulls us forward, yearning for our transformation. Spirit-guides eagerly await the opportunity to help us move forward in life-giving ways. But ultimately, whether we move forward or stay stuck in the past is a choice we all must make for ourselves. Walt Disney knew this well, and is famous for saying: "We keep moving forward."[94] With her curious nature and pursuit of new adventures, Belle personifies this quote, as does Jesus. Neither Jesus nor Belle is satisfied with just one act of service or one life lesson. They do not rest in one place for very long, nor do they wallow in the ugliness of past troubles or present danger. Both face difficulties with faith and hope, persistence and even stubbornness. They expect as much or more from themselves as they do from others. Always moving forward, they continue on the journey, living the lessons they have learned, even as they embrace new lessons along the way. Keep moving forward. This is a handy habit on the journey toward transformation.

Beauty and the Beast is a story calling us to move toward the life-giving transformation that changes people, communities, and even the world. This is the gospel Jesus embodies and the good news he proclaims. Read any of the gospels, and you will discover that Jesus never stays in one place for long, for there are always more lessons to teach and learn, more people to heal and love, and more opportunities to grow and encourage others. Jesus doesn't just preach against injustice and hypocrisy; he resists injustice and challenges us to be justice-seekers and instruments of love and compassion. Jesus doesn't just talk about a utopian future where we will eat pie in the sky in the sweet bye and bye after we die; Jesus shows us the kingdom of God—a realm that is in our very midst when we feed the hungry, heal the sick, clothe the naked, visit the sick and imprisoned, welcome the stranger, and love the outcast. Jesus doesn't just heal people; he comes to us with unbridled optimism, encouraging us to become our very best selves.

In every word, every act, every lesson, Jesus measures himself against the very law of love that defines his life and ministry. He exemplifies the loving transformation that lies at the heart of the gospels. Jesus is always moving forward to the next act of service, the next opportunity to teach and to learn, the next life-changing encounter. Even when forward movement threatens his very life, Jesus never turns aside, continuing to offer grace to others until the very end. Hanging from the cross, Jesus offers forgiveness to those who condemned him to

134

die, and saving grace to a repentant thief who hangs dying alongside him.

Belle, too, isn't satisfied with saving her father, reveling in her beautiful new palace bedroom, or exulting in the scrumptious meals Beast's servants provide. She has more worlds to explore, more friends to encounter, and more lessons to learn and teach. Even when she has the opportunity to escape Beast in the forest and head home to her father, this action would surely condemn Beast to death and is something that she simply cannot do. Returning to the castle in order to save and care for Beast, Belle seeks to help Beast and his servants overcome the spell on the castle. Settling into her new life, she teaches Beast to befriend animals, appreciate good books, and perceive the beauty of his castle grounds. As Belle comes to know her new friends in the castle, she brings love and joy to each encounter with enchanted servants and newly reformed Beast. The more Belle opens herself to the magic and mystery of the castle, the more expansive her heart, soul, and mind become. The more Belle grows, the more she is moved to help Beast experience this growth for himself.

Belle never stops moving forward. At every stage of her journey, Belle dreams of exploring new frontiers and pushes through the boundaries that would keep her small. This is the heart of the Jesus-journey: To embrace the fullness of life and to keep moving forward on our path toward transformation—a transformation that brings light and love to every life we touch.

THE ADVENTURE IS JUST BEGINNING

The journey toward transformation is an adventure—a road calling us to embrace love and life at ever-deeper levels. As we expand our open-minded perspectives and hope-filled perceptions, the journey forward becomes clearer and more defined. As we embrace this journey with heartfelt gratitude and self-giving love, the life and love within us swell near to bursting. Just as Belle's beautiful spirit reveals the beautiful spirit of a prince trapped in a beast's body, so too our beautiful spirits can reveal the beautiful spirits of others, and vice-versa. Supportive communities help us on our journeys toward transformation, blessing us with insight, encouragement, and the strength to keep moving forward.

As we travel this road together, we add to the indescribable beauty of our world—a world that blesses every living creature with gifts beyond measure. The Source of truth and beauty that permeates all things pulls us upward and onward. And just as Beast's transformation ultimately transforms his entire community, the blessings within our own transformations ripple through our communities like a stone tossed into still waters. Belle and Beast bless their communities in ways simple and profound. We too can bless our communities by embarking on journeys toward transformation and by embracing life-giving change along the way.

As the love between Belle and Beast grows and their faith in one another expands, they create a magic even greater than the spell cast by the enchantress. Likewise, as our love grows and our faith in God and one another expands, we too create the magic of divine love—a magic that connects heaven and earth, a magic that brings the realm of God within our midst. As we ignite hope in others, they too are drawn to join this magical, spiritual journey of transformative love. Together, our creative magic reveals more creative magic; our expansive love generates more expansive love. Just as Beast, Belle, and their communities are bound together within a common story, so too are we bound together within a common story—a story where love and hope strengthen both personal and communal journeys toward transformation.

Sometimes, we are given the miraculous opportunity to be instruments of divine intervention—sparking the light of hope, as Belle did for Beast; opening new worlds for another, as Beast did for Belle; guiding and encouraging others along the way, as the servants did for both of our heroes. In the end, there was not just one savior in this story; there never is. Belle saves Beast; Beast saves Belle; Beast saves the castle community at the same time the castle community saves Beast and Belle. And while this is playing out, all are strengthened by the magical power of transformative love; all are helped along by a mysterious spiritual guide—seldom seen, but present nevertheless. In the end, these beloved fairytale characters save one another as surely as they are saved. So it is with our stories of transformation as well. Through the power of transformative love, we save one another as surely as we are being saved.

Could there be a better resolution to our stories? Could there be a more fitting remembrance to our lives than that we spent our days well: saving others, and being saved; transforming the broken hearted and being transformed; blessing the weak and the needy, and being blessed by them in turn? Truly, this is a fairytale ending to pray and work for. Truly the realm of God will be in our midst when each and every inhabitant on earth can say: "Love has transformed me; and through me, love has transformed the world." May we trust in this love. May we embrace the light within. And may we always see clearly, so that we recognize this truth: Beauty is all around. Beauty is within. Beauty is.

ENDNOTES

¹ Gibran, Kahlil. "On Children" from *The Prophet*. 1923.

² Woolverton, Linda, screenplay writer. *Beauty and the Beast*. Walt Disney Pictures, 1991.

³ 1 John 4:8

⁴ *Beauty and the Beast*. 2017 Walt Disney Pictures and Mandeville Films. This verse of poetry was likely inspired by the poetry of William Sharp, which Belle reads to Beast beforehand. Sharp's beautiful poem from *A Crystal Forest, mid 1800s) Selected Writings of Wm Sharp, Vol. 1, Poems, TRANSCRIPTS FROM NATURE (FROM "THE HUMAN INHERITANCE" AND "EARTH'S VOICES") 1882-1886* reads:

> The air is blue and keen and cold
> And in a frozen sheeth enrolled
> Each branch, each twig, each blade of grass
> Seems clad miraculously in glass

⁵ Torah can refer to all of traditional Jewish learning, but "the Torah" usually refers to the written Torah, also known as the Chumash (the five volumes or Pentateuch, sometimes referred to as the Five Books of Moses). Hillel, a famous sage of ancient Judaism, is oft-quoted for expressing the golden rule as the summary of all of Torah in the *Babylonian Talmud*, Shabbat 31a.

⁶ Mark 7:15, 20-21, 23

⁷ Matthew 23:25, 27-28

⁸ Rohr, Richard. *Falling Upward: A Spirituality for the Two Halves of Life*. © 2011 Richard Rohr. Published by Jossey-Bass

⁹ Matthew 6:19-21 and Matthew 16:23

¹⁰ 1 Corinthians 1:18-25

¹¹ John 10:10

¹² Matthew 14:29-31

[13] Read the full story of this unusual experience in Acts 2:1-20.

[14] Thoreau, Henry David. *Walden* or *Life in the Woods*. 1854.

[15] Woolverton, Linda, screenplay writer. *Beauty and the Beast*. Walt Disney Pictures, 1991.

[16] Geisel, Theodor Seuss. *How the Grinch Stole Christmas*. © 1957 and 1985 Dr. Seuss Enterprises, L.P.

[17] Mark 10:15

[18] Luke 7:36-50

[19] Luke 2:7 indicates there was no guest room available for Joseph and Mary, as she prepared to give birth. Matthew 2:13 indicates that an angel warns Joseph to flee with his new wife and baby to safety in Egypt, away from the threat that King Herod is seeking to kill the baby Jesus.

[20] Luke 10:25-37

[21] Matthew 7:20

[22] Matthew 25:43. Or read the full *Parable of the Sheep and the Goats* by reading Verses 31-46 of Chapter 25 in *The Gospel According to Matthew*.

[23] Read the full story in The Gospel of John, Chapter 9, verses 1-41.

[24] Matthew 6:25-34

[25] Shakespeare, William. *Hamlet*. Late 16th century.

[26] Einstein, Albert. Statement to William Miller, from the memoirs of William Miller, an editor, quoted in Life magazine, May 2, 1955; Expanded, p. 281. Full quote: "The important thing is not to stop questioning. Curiosity has its own reason for existing. One cannot help but be in awe when he contemplates the mysteries of eternity, of life, of the marvelous structure of reality. It is enough if one tries merely to comprehend a little of this mystery every day. Never lose a holy curiosity."

[27] Mark 2:27

[28] Matthew 5:13-14

[29] While a sign points to something that is absent, a symbol re-presents something that is actually present.

[30] Mark 7:18, 20

[31] Luke 18:15-17

[32] Carroll, Lewis. *Through the Looking Glass, and What Alice Found There.* 1871.

[33] Ephesians 1:17-18a, paraphrase.

[34] de Saint-Exupéry, Antoine. *The Little Prince.* Translated from the French by Katherine Woods. ©1943 and 1971 Harcourt Brace Jovanovich, Inc.

[35] John 11:41b; Matthew 11:25; Matthew 14:13-21; Mark 6:30-43; Luke 9:10-17; 1 Corinthians 11:23-26.

[36] *Beauty and the Beast.* 2017 Walt Disney Pictures and Mandeville Films.

[37] Shakespeare, William. *A Midsummer Night's Dream.* Act 1, Scene 1. 1596.

[38] Townshend, Pete. "Let My Love Open the Door," *Empty Glass*, Atco Records, 1980.

[39] Henri Nouwen, "SILENCE: On Words and Silence," from *The Way of the Heart.* © 1981 Henri Nouwen.

[40] Matthew 5:8

[41] 1 Corinthians 13; 1 John; 2 John; 3 John

[42] John 15:13

[43] Woolverton, Linda, screenplay writer. *Beauty and the Beast.* Walt Disney Pictures, 1991.

[44] Ashman, Howard, lyricist. "Beauty and the Beast" from Walt Disney's *Beauty and the Beast.* © 1991 Walt Disney Music Company and Wonderland Music Company, Inc.

[45] Woolverton, Linda, screenplay writer. *Beauty and the Beast.* Walt Disney Pictures, 1991.

[46] John 15:13

[47] Ephesians 5:22-25. See especially Verses 22 and 25, which read: "Wives, submit yourselves to your own husbands as you do to the Lord…. Husbands, love your wives, just as Christ loved the church and gave himself up for her."

[48] Luke 19:1-10

[49] Matthew 27:54

[50] Kloves, Steve, screenwriter and J. K. Rowling, author. *Harry Potter and the Sorcerer's Stone.* 2001, Warner Bros., Heydey Films and 1492 Pictures.

[51] Mark 15:4

[52] Matthew 27:24b

[53] John 1:1-9

[54] Bono and the Edge, "Song for Someone," *Songs of Innocence*, © 2014 Island Records

[55] An adaptation of Jesus' teaching of Hillel's "Golden Rule": "Do to others what you would have others do to you" (Luke 6:31).

[56] Woolverton, Linda, screenplay writer. *Beauty and the Beast.* Walt Disney Pictures, 1991.

[57] *The Lion King.* Walt Disney Pictures, 1994.

[58] Woolverton, Linda, screenplay writer. *Beauty and the Beast.* Walt Disney Pictures, 1991.

[59] In John 15:15, Jesus says: "I no longer call you servants, because a servant does not know his master's business. Instead, I have called you friends."

[60] Julian of Norwich. *Revelations of Divine Love.* 1395. Her original Middle English quote states, "For in the Beholding of God we fall not, and in the beholding of self we stand not."

[61] Matthew 23:37; Luke 13:34

[62] The Parable of the Talents can be found in Matthew 25:14-30.

[63] From 1 John 4:18

[64] Woolverton, Linda, screenplay writer. *Beauty and the Beast.* Walt Disney Pictures, 1991.

[65] John 11:35

[66] Ezekiel 37:1-14

[67] Paul writes of this same idea in Romans 8:23, reminding that the entire creation community yearns for transformation into the world God intends for us to be and become.

[68] *Beauty and the Beast.* 2017 Walt Disney Pictures and Mandeville Films.

[69] Woolverton, Linda, screenplay writer. *Beauty and the Beast.* Walt Disney Pictures, 1991.

[70] Ashman, Howard, lyricist. "Something There," from Walt Disney's *Beauty and the Beast.* © 1991 Walt Disney Music Company and Wonderland Music Company, Inc.

[71] Genesis 2:18-24

[72] Ecclesiastes 4:9

[73] Matthew 18:20

[74] Luke 4:29

[75] Mark 6:4

[76] Woolverton, Linda, screenplay writer. *Beauty and the Beast.* Walt Disney Pictures, 1991.

[77] Ashman, Howard, lyricist. "Belle," from Walt Disney's *Beauty and the Beast.* © 1991 Walt Disney Music Company and Wonderland Music Company, Inc.

[78] Woolverton, Linda, screenplay writer. *Beauty and the Beast.* Walt Disney Pictures, 1991.

[79] Luke 3:23 tells us that "Jesus was about 30 years old when he began his work."

[80] This is a non-scriptural story of Jesus' early life, dating from the 2nd century, likely written to satisfy a yearning to hear more miraculous stories of Jesus' childhood. Scholars agree that it was not written by the disciple Thomas.

[81] Ashman, Howard, lyricist. "Belle (Reprise)," from Walt Disney's *Beauty and the Beast.* © 1991 Walt Disney Music Company and Wonderland Music Company, Inc.

[82] Ashman, Howard, lyricist. "Gaston," from Walt Disney's *Beauty and the Beast.* © 1991 Walt Disney Music Company and Wonderland Music Company, Inc.

[83] Ashman, Howard, lyricist. "Be Our Guest," from Walt Disney's *Beauty and the Beast.* © 1991 Walt Disney Music Company and Wonderland Music Company, Inc.

[84] Thurman, Howard. "Christmas is Waiting to be Born," *The Mood of Christmas and Other Celebrations.* © 1973 Harper and Row.

[85] Hillel, *Babylonian Talmud,* Shabbat 31a

[86] According to Matthew 17:2, Mark 9:2, and Luke 9:29, Jesus was transfigured on a mountaintop, filled with a radiant light shining from his face and clothed in robes as white as lightning. Heavenly visages of Elijah and Moses appear in conversation beside him during this transfiguration experience.

[87] Ashman, Howard, lyricist. "Beauty and the Beast" from Walt Disney's *Beauty and the Beast.* © 1991 Walt Disney Music Company and Wonderland Music Company, Inc.

[88] This statement is found in the Midrash Rabba, Bereshit 10:6.

[89] Lao Tzu, *Tao Te Ching,* 6th century B.C., English transliteration 1891.

[90] Learn more about the story of the poppies at http://www.greatwar.co.uk/article/remembrance-poppy.htm.

[91] Matthew 19:21

[92] Isaiah 40:3

[93] Truly, God is closer to us than our very breath and moves within us with such subtlety (most of the time), we are unaware of the Spirit's gentle guidance.

[94] Disney, Walt. Credited at the end of Walt Disney's *Meet the Robinsons,* Walt Disney Films, 2007. The full quote states, "Around here, however, we don't look backwards for very long. We keep moving forward, opening up new doors and doing new things, because we're curious... and curiosity keeps leading us down new paths."

ABOUT THE AUTHOR

As an individual and corporate consultant with an emphasis on the powerful gifts that creativity, change and transformation bring to individuals and communities, Mary Scifres brings her inspirational outlook and energetic leadership to speaking engagements, writing, teaching, and coaching. Mary's engaging, relational style helps audiences and clients explore personal and institutional change. Her passion is contagious, as is her vision of change as a friendly companion—an ever-present companion brimming with limitless possibilities on our journeys toward transformation. Most of all, Mary inspires people who are inspiring others and working to make the world a better place.

A graduate of Boston University and the University of Indianapolis, Mary Scifres is an ordained United Methodist pastor who has penned hundreds of sermons and dozens of worship resource books over the last 25 years. Mary is the author of *Searching for Seekers: Ministry with a New Generation of the Unchurched* and *Just in Time! Special Services.* For the past twenty-seven years, Mary has co-authored annual publications of *Prepare!: An Ecumenical Music and Worship Planner* and *The United Methodist Music and Worship Planner* with David Bone. And for the past fifteen years, Mary has co-edited *The Abingdon Worship Annual* with her husband, B. J. Beu for Abingdon Press. The two have recently published *Is It Communion Sunday Already?! Communion Resources for All Seasons* through Amazon. Finally, Mary pens several on-line resources each month that are available through her website at maryscifres.com.

To reach Mary for speaking engagements or book signings, email maryscifres@gmail.com. Learn more about Mary's work by visiting maryscifres.com.

Made in the USA
Middletown, DE
13 February 2018